Joanne's gold bracelets clanged together like a death knell—mine. "We'd love to have you, Megan," she said. "We're always looking for volunteers."

My fate was sealed. I pictured myself in a red-and-white furry outfit with matching boots and tassels. I pictured thousands of little kids about to enter the Temple of Santa with me as their leader. I pictured the smile I would have to locate deep within my somber personality. And then I prayed that no one from Carlton Middle School or my neighborhood or anywhere I had ever been in my entire life would show up—especially not Trevor Harris.

Confessions

For Dad, the best Santa ever
—P. McB.

For information address
Hyperion Books for Children,
114 Fifth Avenue, New York, New York, 10011.

A Hyperion Paperback original

First edition: October 1994
1   3   5   7   9   10   8   6   4   2

Library of Congress Cataloging-in-Publication Data

McBrier, Page.
Confessions of a reluctant elf/Page McBrier—1st ed.
p.   cm.
Summary: As a reluctant member of a Christmas-obsessed family,
Megan has a bad case of the bah-humbugs until she befriends a
runaway boy hiding out in the store where she works as Santa's elf.
ISBN 0-7868-1010-6 (pbk.)
[1. Christmas—Fiction.   2. Runaways—Fiction.
3. Family life—Fiction.   4. Department stores—Fiction.]   I. Title.
PZ7.M4783Co   1994
[Fic]—dc20
94-8006 CIP AC

Chapter One

My parents call me the Scrooge of Lilac Lane, but to everyone else I'm Megan Gallagher. And to set the record straight, I like Christmas. It's just that every year since I can remember, Dad has spent the month of December playing head Santa at T. D. Hocker's department store, and I have to tell you that once he switches from Ed Gallagher, shoe department, to Ed Gallagher, Santa Land, it gets so jolly around here even the Pillsbury doughboy would have a hard time keeping up.

Take this morning, for instance. Breakfast at 30 Lilac Lane, December 6, 7:30 A.M. "Ho, ho, ho," said you know who, coming into the kitchen in his blue-and-white terry-cloth robe with Hilton Hotels embroidered across the pocket. (Contrary to what you might think, you don't need a white beard and potbelly to be hired as Santa.)

I stared into my Rice Krispies.

"And how are Santa's big helpers this morning?" Dad continued.

"Fine," said Mom and I. Until this fall, my sister, Sarah, was among the big helpers, but she has escaped to college.

Dad helped himself to a huge bowl of cereal and then hummed "Deck the Halls" while heaping on the sugar. "Busy day ahead," he announced. "I'm scheduled to be on the floor from ten to six. Then the store is sending me over to the Becker Building to make an appearance at the Retailers Association Christmas party." He grinned at Mom. "How about you?"

"Just another day at Ivy Manor," she said, smiling back. When Sarah went off to college, Mom got a job at a nearby nursing home to help pay her tuition.

Now came the killer. "So, Megan. Got any plans for after school?" asked Dad.

I could tell by the glint in his eye that if I didn't, he did. "Not really," I said, bracing myself.

"I could use your help at the Christmas party, passing out candy canes and key chains."

I quickly swallowed my spoonful of Rice Krispies so I wouldn't choke. "I don't think so, Dad. I'm not into elves lately."

He gave me a surprised look. "What are you talking about! What's Christmas without elves? Nothing, that's what. And the only requirement for an elf is a smile. Right, Anne?"

"Right," said Mom, showing us hers.

I slid my chair back from the table. "It's . . . it's not for me, Dad. Sorry."

Dad got up and slouched over to the sink with his cereal bowl. I could tell that his feelings were hurt.

"Megan, are you sure?" asked Mom softly, leaning toward me. Her personalized Christmas ornament earrings swung back and forth.

I lowered my voice. "Mom, seventh graders don't usually spend much time with Santa. We're supposed to have outgrown him by now."

"But it's not Santa," she whispered back. "It's Dad. And it would mean a lot to him if you took some interest. . . ." She leaned closer. "Just this once?"

So that's how I ended up here, outside the Becker Building, freezing my rear off while I waited for Dad to pull into the partially hidden parking spot I'd scoped out. T. D. Hocker's has very strict rules about its Santas, one of them being that Santa is never to be seen getting in or out of a car. Bad for the sleigh image.

Dad finally finished maneuvering, and I walked over to our car. "Ho, ho, ho. Merry Christmas," he said, carefully freeing his pillow belly from behind the steering wheel.

"Dad, it's only me."

He wagged his finger. "I'm not your Dad! I'm Santa Claus!"

I sighed. I heard once that at Buckingham Palace in London, where the queen of England lives, the guards aren't supposed to smile or talk to people. Tourists spend hours trying to get them to break down and act regular. That's sort of the way it is with Dad once he puts on his costume. No matter how hard you try, he won't admit to being anybody but Santa Claus.

We headed toward the building, with Dad waving big hellos to everyone in the parking lot. Once inside, he sprang into action. "M-E-E-E-R-R-R-Y Christmas, folks!" he bellowed, making a beeline for the center of the room.

I waited in a corner, hoping my jean skirt

and brown hair would blend in with the wallpaper. One thing I had refused to go along with was the elf costume. But it wasn't long before I heard a familiar voice saying, "Where's my big helper?"

Here's another thing that bothers me: Other than my long legs, which are recent (due to a growth spurt over the summer), I happen to be small for my age. I take after my mother, the runt of her family. I rushed to Dad's side before he could get into a more detailed description of his "big helper."

All around me people were holding drinks in paper cups and laughing. Dad seated himself in a big comfy chair, obviously placed there for him. Right away, a two-hundred-pound lady in a tight green dress plopped herself down on his lap.

"Ooomph," said Dad, but not too loudly. The lady's drink splashed on his Santa suit. "Hello there," he said, jolly as ever. "What can Santa bring you this year?"

"A raise," she said, cracking up. Everyone thought she was hilarious. Dad laughed, too, and the lady planted a greasy red kiss on his cheek.

I was grossed out, but Dad didn't seem to mind. He never does—that's what bugs me.

Kids pee on him and barf on him and pick at his fake beard, grown-ups give him kisses and pile onto his lap two and three at a time, and still he loves his job. Every year, he can't wait until Christmastime.

The woman standing next to me asked my name.

"That's Sparkle, my head elf," said Dad, before I had a chance to answer. "Isn't she something?" Dad reached around the lady to hand me his Santa sack. "Sparkle, honey? Do we have any key chains and candy canes in there?"

My cheeks did a slow burn as I handed the woman her loot. I tried to imagine I was somewhere else—like in my room, alone.

"Here, honey, put this on," said Dad, handing me a dumb red-and-white elf hat. I balled it up in my hand.

In the corner, a group of people had started a sing-along, and the next thing I knew, Dad and the fat lady were dancing around the room to "Rudolph the Red-Nosed Reindeer."

"Come on, Sparkle, join in," Dad called as they twirled past.

"Uh, I don't think so. . . ."

"You sure?" he said on his next twirl.

I edged myself closer to the Santa

throne. "Positive." I reached into the sack for more candy canes, then waited, still as a statue, for Dad to finish his dance. I figured if I just stood quietly all night, people might forget I was there.

Eighty-five candy canes later, on our way back to Hocker's, Dad and I had a chance to talk in the car while we recovered from our evening. It's true we don't get to see much of each other during the holidays, which is probably why he liked having me around tonight.

"So? Did you have fun?" Dad turned the air conditioner on full blast to cool himself off, even though it was thirty-two degrees outside.

"It was okay."

"But you did such a great job! You have a terrific smile and a wonderful sense of humor. Did you know that? You should give yourself some credit once in a while. Good elves are tough to find."

Darn! I was trying *not* to smile. Who ever saw a smiling statue? I looked down at my lap. "Uh, Dad. I mean, Santa?" I had something to ask him that he probably wouldn't like, and since he was in his suit and I'd just done a good deed, now was the perfect time.

We stopped for a light. In the next car, a

little boy saw Dad and started freaking out.

"What is it, Megan?" said Dad, unrolling his window to wave. According to T. D. Hocker's rules, if you're recognized, acknowledge. "My sleigh's broken," he yelled. The little boy was so excited his face turned the color of an eggplant. The light changed, and Dad did a very loud "MER-R-R-R-Y Christmas!"

"It's about my Christmas presents," I said, sliding down in my seat. "I was wondering if I could get money this year instead."

Dad almost ran off the road. "Money? Santa doesn't bring money! The whole point of presents is that Santa takes the time to select something that he thinks you'll like."

I wanted to tell him that when Mom (aka Santa) selects what she thinks I'll like I usually don't. Instead I said, "I'm saving up for something educational."

That got him. "No kidding! What? A computer?"

I took a breath. "No. Scuba-diving lessons. And you have to have your own equipment."

Dad was quiet for about three blocks. "Is there a lot of scuba diving going on in the greater Indianapolis area?" he asked finally.

I sighed. I wanted to tell him about this idea I had that I would go down to the Florida

Keys someday and swim with the tropical fish. I'd been thinking about it ever since I watched a TV special on underwater exploration and realized how peaceful and beautiful it must be. Underwater tranquility wasn't exactly Dad's thing, though, so I wasn't sure how he'd react.

We pulled into the alley behind Hocker's and parked beside the loading dock. "We'll talk more later," Dad said, patting my hand.

He made sure no one was around before hopping out of the car. Then together we rode the freight elevator up to Santa Land.

T. D. Hocker's Santa Land has been around for sixty years, making it something of an institution. And it's not just Santa that people come to see. It's the whole Santa environment that Hocker's creates.

First, this is not your typical mall Santa setup. No way. Except for the Tea Room, the *entire* sixth floor is taken over. As you get off the elevator, you're greeted by giant animated displays of cozy Christmas scenes, like teddy bears drinking hot chocolate and reindeer wrapping gifts. At the actual entrance to Santa Land, there's a miniature train only kids can fit into waiting to take you on a magic ride through the North Pole. You climb in, wave good-bye to your parents, and ride in circles around the sixth floor, past more mechanical elves and North Pole creatures who wave and sing Christmas songs.

When the train finally stops at Santa's Gingerbread House, an elf is waiting with your parents to lead you inside. After you've had your picture taken and told Santa what you want for Christmas, you're ushered back out the door and through the exit, where Mrs. Claus is waiting to hand you a candy cane. And that's not all: down on the fifth floor you can visit Oswald, the talking bear; the Story Lady; and the decorate-your-own-Christmas-cookie table.

I have to admit that when I was a little kid, I loved it here. Who wouldn't? People who came here as children now bring their *own* children. Coming to Hocker's to see Santa has become an annual event in Indianapolis. . . . Would you believe last year they had more than fifty-five thousand visitors?

Enough is enough, though. After twelve years of hanging around Santa Land, and especially after tonight's one-elf experience, I had to let Dad know I didn't want to do the duty again. Ever.

"Hi, Santa," said a nicely dressed woman with red hair as we got off the freight elevator. "How'd it go?"

"Great, just great," said Dad. He actually meant it. "Joanne, do you remember Megan?"

"Gosh, you've grown up," said this person I never remembered meeting.

"Joanne's in charge of Special Promotions," said Dad. "If it weren't for her, there wouldn't *be* a Santa Land."

Joanne flashed a set of perfect teeth. "We couldn't do it without your dad, though," she said. "He's our number one Santa, aren't you, Ed?"

Dad let out one of his better ho, ho, hos. "Megan helped me out tonight at the Retailers Association."

"Terrific!" said Joanne. "It must run in the family!"

Dad beamed. "You're right. In fact, I was thinking maybe we could find a permanent spot for her here."

My throat closed. My stomach did a nosedive. Me? The Scrooge of Lilac Lane? A full-time elf? He must be kidding. "I . . ."

Joanne's gold bracelets clanged together like a death knell—mine. "We'd love to have you, Megan," she said. "We're always looking for volunteers."

"But I—"

"Why don't you think about it?"

She smiled. Dad smiled. "It'd be a chance to spend some time together," said Dad. "Sarah helped out one Christmas when she was about your age, remember?"

Oh, sure. Sarah the perfect. My fate was sealed. I pictured myself in a red-and-white furry outfit with matching boots and tassels. I pictured thousands of little kids about to enter the Temple of Santa with me as their leader. I pictured the smile I would have to locate deep within my somber personality. And then I prayed that no one from Carlton Middle School or my neighborhood or anywhere I had ever been in my entire life would show up— especially not Trevor Harris.

Chapter Two

Let me tell you about Trevor Harris. Besides being the cutest boy in the eighth grade, he actually knows who I am. I got this information from my best friend, Jennifer Parkes. At her house not long ago, waiting for our bean burritos to come out of the microwave, she told me, "Trevor came up to me in the lunch line today and said, 'Your friend Megan sure is dumb.'"

I was flattered. Then I thought about it. "What do you mean, *dumb*?"

The microwave beeped. "He thinks you don't know how to ride a bike."

"Just because I ran into him?" I said. "How else was I supposed to get him to remember me? Besides, I was only going two miles an hour."

Jennifer rolled her eyes. "Why do you

13

want to bother with Trevor, anyway? Every girl in school likes him."

"I know." I watched Jennifer slice our burritos in half. "Maybe I shouldn't have hit him so hard."

Jennifer laughed so much she sent the steam from our burritos billowing across the room in tiny cloud formations. "Megan, you slay me," she said. Jennifer's always coming up with unusual vocabulary words like "slay."

I took a bite of my burrito and frowned. Why was it everyone except me thought I was so funny?

Anyway, that's Trevor Harris. And you can see what I mean about not wanting to be seen in an elf costume. So as soon as Dad and I were out of Joanne's earshot I tried *desperately* to get out of elf patrol. I pleaded homework overload. I pleaded early Christmas burnout. No dice. Dad was so excited to have me on board, his ears must not have been working. I decided to try again later, when Mom was around to stick up for me.

We reached the Santa dressing room. "Wait here," said Dad, disappearing inside to change.

Having multiple Santas is one of Hocker's big secrets that no one's supposed to know about. They have six, and because of the number of people who come through Santa Land, three of them are usually on duty at once. The way it's done is to have three separate rooms off a long hallway, each with a Santa waiting inside.

With all those Santas running around, you can imagine what their dressing room looks like. Or maybe you can't. Dad showed it to me once when it was empty. It's not very glamorous—more like one of those depressing group dressing rooms in bargain-basement stores. Each Santa has his own locker, and there's a long makeup table with little pots of rouge and cold cream and boxes of tissues. In the corner a big cardboard box holds the extra pillow bellies. The red suits are hung on a long rack by the far wall, with cardboard name tags on the hangers to keep them from getting mixed up.

"Ready to head home?" said Dad, emerging with one of the other Santas, a short bald guy who needed no pillow. Dad introduced me. "Bob, this is my daughter Megan. She's going to be helping me out this Christmas."

I started feeling desperate again.

Bob bobbed his head. "That's nice," he said in a voice as flat as a dead Coke. (It was then I realized you don't necessarily need a bubbly personality to work on the Santa crew.) He stared at me politely. "When do you start?"

"Um . . ." I tried to stall.

"How 'bout tomorrow?" said Dad, sending my system into shock. "Saturdays are a real zoo around here. Right, Bob-o?"

"I suppose," said Bob-o.

Dad looked over at the schedule, which was posted on the wall outside the dressing room. "I'm slotted for eleven." He glanced at me. "What do you think? Do you have any other plans?"

My mind blanked. "I know there's something," I said weakly.

Dad frowned. "Gee, I hope not. I was looking forward to this."

"I know," I said, sighing. "You told me already."

Mom was no help at all. "Oh, it'll be fun," she said, later that evening. "Why don't you at least try it out?"

"I *did*," I said. "Remember?"

"An office party is entirely different.

Right, Ed?" Dad nodded. Now it was Mom's turn to bring up the Sarah factor. "When Sarah was your age, she didn't want to help out one Christmas, either, and she ended up having a wonderful time." The logic here was that since it happened that way with Sarah, it would happen that way with me, too.

I wanted to explain that Sarah and I were totally different, that Sarah was the outgoing and noisy type, while I was more the shy and sneaky type, but I knew from experience that it would do no good. I was going to have to find another way out. For now I was trapped.

So there I was the next morning, standing in the elf dressing room, preparing to climb into the most hideous costume I'd ever seen. I don't care what Dad says—no one looks good in a red-and-white fur tunic draped over a pair of red tights. To make matters worse, the tunic was one-size-fits-all, and since the elves come in all sizes, it looked like a maternity outfit on me. Luckily, an elf changing nearby said, "There are belts in that box in the corner if you need one."

After gathering up my tunic into accordion pleats, I headed to room three, where I was to get my crash course in elf hospitality from someone named Marge.

I'm not sure where T. D. Hocker's finds all its elves. Some of them are store employees like Dad, and some are in high school and college. I recognized Marge as a refugee from the children's department, a place I'd thankfully outgrown last summer.

"Now, Megan. Let's start when the children first come through the door," said Marge. She sounded like Mr. Rogers in overdrive. "First we *greet* and then we *seat*." With her stout arms she motioned to the huge gold throne. "Try to distribute the children evenly so that Santa doesn't get too squished on one side. Small, large. Small, large. All right?"

She smiled, so I smiled. "Remember," she said, "the children are overexcited. So you need to be on the lookout for catastrophes." She reached behind the throne and pulled out a box of tissues and a roll of paper towels. "Just in case."

Marge went on to show me how to use the Polaroid and then demonstrated a trick for getting everyone's attention. I couldn't believe I was going to spend my Saturday squeaking a little rubber dog over my head.

Once we had the camera technique

down, Marge said, "Now for your most important job." She opened the door to the hallway. "Before you let the children leave, you need to make sure neither of the other Santa doors is opening. It would be a terrible thing to destroy the illusion." She cracked our door a sliver. "*Peek*, then *speak*: 'All right, children. Mrs. Claus is waiting for you at the end of the hall.'" She smiled, I smiled, and Dad walked in.

"Ho, ho, ho."

"Hi, Santa," said Marge. "We were just finishing up."

"Terrific," said Dad. He looked at me. "It's a mob scene out there. You think you're ready?"

"I guess." I could feel my tights sliding down.

"Marge, tell Becky to send in our next customers," said Dad.

I took my place by the throne and gave my tights a good yank. Please, oh, please, I prayed, don't let it be anyone I know.

A family of four—mom, dad, boy, girl—came through the door. "Hello," said Dad.

The little boy burst into tears.

I tried to get him to sit down on Santa's lap. "No," he said, clinging to his mother's leg. "No Santa."

The little girl had already marched herself over to Dad and was rattling off her list. "Uh-huh, uh-huh, uh-huh," Dad said, dabbing his forehead with a handkerchief. "I'll try my best. What about some surprises? Don't you want some surprises?" (Dad never liked to make promises, in case the parents couldn't afford what the kid wanted.)

"Lots of surprises," the little girl said.

Dad looked at me. "Sparkle, how about a picture for our friend Hayley?"

The mother was still trying to pry the boy off her leg. "Conrad, Santa won't hurt you," she said. "He's your friend."

Dad waved. "Hi, Conrad."

Conrad screamed so loud I thought he was going to set off the alarm system.

Dad turned to the mother. "Mom, what do you say we skip Conrad this year?"

By the end of the afternoon I thought I must have seen every type of kid manufactured. We'd had noisy ones, quiet ones, excited ones, frightened ones, even one who bit. And I could already recite the names of the toys they asked for over and over. I was dreaming about the hot-fudge pecan-ball sundae Dad had promised to buy me when there came a knock at the door, signaling our last customer of the day.

A guy walked in. Alone. He was about my age, and skinny, with a pale face and brown hair that poked up in front. He didn't look healthy—more like someone who had survived on a diet of Twinkies and Cokes his entire life. He was wearing jeans, a T-shirt, and a thin jacket. He walked the way boys do when they want to look cool or tough.

"Yo, Santa. How ya doin'?" For such a scrawny-looking person, his voice was surprisingly deep and froggy.

"Just fine," said Dad calmly. "How about you?"

The guy nodded an okay, then checked out me and the room. I moved closer to the throne.

"What's your name?" asked Dad.

"Grady," he said.

"Oh, so *you're* Grady!" Grady looked surprised, and I cringed. I knew what Dad was going to say next. "You're on my good list!"

Grady sort of laughed, but not really. "You work for the store?" he asked Dad.

"When I'm not at the North Pole," Dad

answered in his cheery Santa voice. "What can I bring you for Christmas?"

Grady didn't answer. He moved restlessly around the room like a panther in a cage. "So, how long you been working here?"

"I'm here every Christmas," said Dad.

Grady stopped. "I'm talking about the *real* you."

Dad shifted in his chair. "So am I."

After a minute Grady grinned, breaking the tension. "How many kids you seen today?"

"Oh, I don't know," said Dad. "About five hundred."

"Five hundred! Yo! That's a lot of kids. How long you been sitting here?"

"About six hours," said Dad.

Grady turned and headed for the door. "Well, nice talking to you."

"Wait," said Dad. "Don't you want anything for Christmas?"

But Grady had already slipped out the door.

"That was *weird*," I said.

Dad shrugged. "You see all sorts of people in here."

"What do you think he wanted?"

"Santa," said Dad. He stood up and

stretched. "What do you say we hop on our sleigh and head over to the Tea Room? I'm ready for that hot-fudge pecan-ball sundae."

By the time we got home, it was dark outside. Mom was in the living room, listening to Christmas music and addressing Christmas cards. "How was it?" she asked.

"Tiring," I said.

"Great," Dad said. "Megan does a better job than some of our paid employees."

I cursed the child-labor laws.

"Speaking of paid employees," Mom said, "Sarah called. She got her old job back at the Gourmet Market."

I sighed and chalked up one more for the Christmas fairy. Now I was surrounded. The Gourmet Market is T. D. Hocker's specialty food shop. Sarah worked there two summers during high school.

"That's terrific!" said Dad, giving me a now-we're-all-in-it-together pat. "Maybe she can work her schedule so we can carpool." I squeezed my eyes tight, hoping to block the image of myself hurling down Meridian Boulevard wedged between two maniacs of cheer.

Mom drew a smiling Santa face under her signature on the Christmas card. "By the way, Megan, Jennifer called. She wants you to call her back." Mom slid the card over to me. "Want to write Grammy a little note?"

Under the happy face I put, "Hi, Gram, bye, Gram. Megan."

"Is that it?" said Mom.

I took the card back. "P.S. When are you coming to visit? You can stay in Sarah's room." Mom smiled.

"May I go call Jennifer now?" I asked.

"Where were you all day?" asked Jennifer.

Luckily for me, no one at school knows about my father's other identity. When I was younger, I promised Dad I'd keep it a secret so I wouldn't disappoint anyone who still believed. As I got older I was too embarrassed to tell. I hadn't even told Jennifer, although lately I'd been feeling guilty about that, since she *is* my best friend and all. "Um, downtown. At Hocker's. With Dad."

"Sounds boring," said Jennifer.

The faces of a hundred little kids blew past me. "So, what did you call about?"

"They're doing *Amahl and the Night Visitors* at St. Luke's—and guess who's playing Amahl?"

I didn't want to seem ignorant, but I had

no idea what she was talking about. "What's Amahl?"

"*You* know. It's the old opera about a crippled boy who rides with the Three Wise Men to see the baby Jesus."

"Oh."

"So, who do you think is playing the crippled boy?"

"I don't know. . . ."

"Trevor Harris!"

I gasped. "You mean I crippled him?"

Jennifer cracked up. "You should be a comedian," she said. "Really. You should go on TV."

How could I tell her I was serious?

"So, do you want to get tickets to go see him?" Jennifer said. I liked the idea immediately. It was another chance for Trevor to notice me . . . in a more normal way.

"I'll have to ask Mom. When is it?"

Jennifer gave me the details; Mom gave me the permission.

That night I dreamed I was playing the part of a shepherd in *Amahl and the Night Visitors*. I was backstage with Trevor and had just offered to adjust his crutches before he had to make his next entrance. "Are you crazy?" he shouted in front of everyone. "Keep your mitts off me."

I was about to defend myself when suddenly I heard, "Ho, ho, ho, rise and shine, Sparkle!"

My head shot off the pillow.

"And how is my number one elf this morning?" said Dad, looming over me in his bathrobe.

Trevor's crutches hobbled away. "Okay, I guess."

"How'd you like to help me out in the Tea Room this morning? I've got five hundred people coming for Breakfast with Santa."

I must have groaned, although I don't remember it.

"Are you feeling all right?" asked Dad.

I sat up and rubbed my eyes. "Yeah. What about Sunday school?"

"Santa's giving special permission to miss it this week."

"Oh." I closed my eyes and actually tried to wish myself back into my dream. All of a sudden my Trevor nightmare didn't seem nearly as bad as the Santa nightmare I was about to face.

Chapter Three

Remember that weird kid Grady? I saw him again today. He came into the room where Dad and I were working after Breakfast with Santa.

"Well, well, well. You again?" said Dad when he saw him coming through the door.

Grady's face stretched into a strange smile. "How 'bout that?" he said, obviously pleased with himself. "They wanted to send me through door three, but I held out for two. I knew you were in two today." He walked over and gave Dad a high five. "So how you doin'?"

"Great!" said Dad. "Couldn't be better. How about you?"

Instead of answering, Grady stepped behind the camera and peered through the lens at us. "Smile, folks."

"How did you know where we were?" I asked, forgetting about T. D. Hocker's rule of elf silence.

Grady leaned around the side of the camera and grinned. "I'm psychic. Ha, ha, ha." He put his eye up to the lens again. "This job doesn't look too hard."

"It isn't," I said in my politest voice. "All you need is half a brain."

The camera clicked.

"Gotcha!" said Grady. He pulled back from the camera and started pacing the room again, like he had done the day before. "So, how long did you say you've been working here?" he asked Dad.

"I always spend a few weeks at Hocker's before heading back to the Pole," said Dad in his Santa voice.

Grady shook his head. "Tough to crack."

Dad grinned. "Just doing my job, son."

"Hmph." Grady crossed the room and took the picture out of the camera. "Your mouth was open," he said, handing it to me. His eyes slid sideways. "Looks like *you* got half a brain."

"Ha, ha. Very funny."

Dad cleared his throat. "So, Grady, you still haven't told Santa what you'd like for Christmas."

Grady spun around. "How old do you think I am? Take a guess. I just had another birthday."

Dad continued in his Santa mode. "People of all ages come to see Santa."

"Eleven," I said through my teeth.

"Eleven!" Grady shouted. He started hopping up and down like Rumpelstiltskin. "You think I look eleven? For your information, I happen to be fourteen years old. Fourteen and counting."

"No way."

"Yes way. Why? How old are you?" He looked me over one more time. "Eight?"

"Eight!" I pulled at my elf tunic. "You can't be serious."

"Kids, kids," said Dad. "Enough!"

"But Dad!" I said—and then froze.

Grady cocked his head to one side. *"Dad?"*

Now I'd done it. I'd blown my cover. Dad was going to murder me.

"I *thought* something was up," said Grady, circling the Santa throne like a vulture. "You don't look old enough to work here."

"I'm a volunteer," I said.

"Grady," interrupted Dad, "other people are waiting to see Santa. Is there anything you'd like to ask before you leave?"

Grady's eyes darted around the room before landing back on Dad. "Yeah." He pointed at Dad's huge gold chair. "Where'd you get that thing? I could use one for my room."

Dad guffawed loudly and patted the chair's arm. "You like this, huh? I picked it up at a Vatican garage sale."

"Oh brother," I said under my breath.

The two of them cracked up. "Ha, ha, ha," said Grady, holding his sides. "Holy moly. A Vatican garage sale. I like that." He calmed down enough to saunter to the door. "You're one funny dude," he said, then pointed to me. "You, too, if you'd lighten up."

"Ooooh," I said, clenching my fists.

The minute the door closed, Dad said, "Is there any reason you were so unfriendly, Sparkle?" I knew he called me by my elf name to remind me of my responsibilities.

"What does he want?" I answered. "He's too old for Santa. Why's he bothering you?"

"I'm not sure," said Dad, "but getting yourself all worked up won't help." He looked down at the picture Grady took of us and chuckled. "You know, honey, the trick to being a good Santa is knowing when to listen. I bet if we give Grady half a chance, he'll tell us in his own way what he's after."

Our shift finally ended at five o'clock. I couldn't believe how tired I was. It was like I'd had five

PE classes and a track meet all in a row. "I'll wait for you on the sofas by the Tea Room," I told Dad, dragging myself out the elf door.

"Deal," said Dad. He still sounded cheerful. The man is incredible.

Inside the dressing room, I quickly pulled off my tunic and tossed it into the dirty tunic box. Yuck! Only three more weeks of red polyester to go.

I finished getting dressed and hurried out to the sofas. "Ahhh." My body sank deep into the cushions.

Suddenly a bony hand holding a giant can of popcorn dropped in front of my face.

"Want some?"

I looked behind me. It was that Grady kid again. "What do *you* want?"

"Nothing. I'm offering you some popcorn."

I turned my head. "No thanks. I'm not hungry."

He jiggled the can back and forth. "Bubblegum flavor. It's good for you."

I looked at him again. "Since when is bubblegum good for you?"

"Since . . . I don't know." He shrugged. "Maybe it has fluoride in it." That cracked him up. "Ha, ha, ha. Bubblegum popcorn with fluoride. Ha, ha."

I smiled politely.

Without waiting for an invitation, Grady hopped over the back of the sofa and plopped down beside me. "So how come you hate being an elf?"

I scooched way over. "I never said I hated it."

He gave me this all-knowing smile. "There's something you don't like about it, though, isn't there? Admit it."

This guy was getting to me. "Listen . . ."

"Ready to go, Megan?"

Oh great. There was Father Christmas, standing in his street clothes at the end of the sofa.

Immediately Grady shot out of his seat. "Yo, Santa!"

Dad spun 360 degrees. "Santa's here? Where?"

I rolled my eyes. Grady still didn't get it. He said to Dad, "No, no. We met already, re-member? Twice. In room two and room three. Grady Watkins."

Dad played stumped. "I don't know what you're talking about. I'm Ed Gallagher. I work in Ladies' Shoes."

Grady paused and then leaned over to me. "Is he serious?" he whispered.

I wanted to sink into the sofa and drown. "Just go along with him, will you?"

Grady shrugged and straightened back up. "Okay. Nice meeting you . . . Ed. Heh, heh."

I stood up stiffly.

"You, too, *Megan.*" He bent toward my ear. "I see what you mean . . . kinda corny, isn't he?"

I couldn't make it to the elevators fast enough.

Later that evening, Jennifer called. "Do you have plans next Saturday?" she asked.

I twisted the phone cord around my little finger.

"Why?"

"I thought we could go shopping for Christmas presents together."

Thump, thump, thump. My heart banged against my ribs. "Where?"

"I don't know. Maybe we could get a ride with your dad down to Hocker's. Have you ever been to their Santa Land?"

"Not since I was little," I said, crossing my fingers so I wouldn't be jinxed for lying. "Besides, Dad's not working Saturday."

"So let's go to the mall," said Jennifer. "I hear it's spectacular."

"Can't."

"Why not?"

"Ummmm." I sort of wanted to tell Jennifer the truth, but something told me to hold off. She sometimes has a big mouth. One time she announced in front of our entire Girl Scout troop that my bra looked lopsided. "Ummm. I promised my mom I'd help put up the tree." I crossed my fingers again and hoped Jennifer wouldn't remember that in the House of Christmas, our decorations go up the day after Thanksgiving, just like the department stores'.

"Oh. Well, okay."

Luckily, Mom started calling me to come help with the dinner dishes, so I had a good excuse to get off the phone.

"Who was that, sweetie?" Mom asked, handing me a Frosty the Snowman dish towel.

"Jennifer."

Mom smiled. "She's a nice friend, isn't she?"

I picked a piece of food crud off the holly casserole dish. "I hope so," I said, leaving it at that.

* * *

Every night that week Dad came home with another Grady story to tell. I guess Dad and I weren't the only people he was being friendly to. Would you believe he came into Santa Land six times that week? By Wednesday, he knew all the elves by name and had even talked Mrs. Claus into letting him help hand out candy canes. Here's the really strange part, though. Each time he knew exactly where to find Dad. *And* he told Dad he knew he was the head Santa, as if that were important.

So when we started our shift on Saturday, I kind of thought we'd run into Grady, only we didn't. Instead we'd been doing our Christmas-cheer act all morning and were about to break for lunch when in he sailed.

"Yo, Santa," he said, pretending to box his way across the room. He gave me an imaginary bop on the arm. "You, too, Tinker Bell."

I narrowed my eyes. "It's Sparkle."

He shrugged. "What's the difference? You don't sparkle *or* twinkle."

Before I had a chance to defend myself, Dad interrupted. "Nice to see you today, Grady."

Grady shoved his hands into his jacket pockets and then took them out again. "Yeah." He started his darting eyes routine. "So tell me something. That kid out there who's driving the Santa train. How old is he?"

"You mean James?" said Dad. "I think he's about fifteen."

Grady nodded, like he already knew the answer. "See there? *About* fifteen. Just like me." He glanced around the room again. "So, doesn't he ever get a break?"

"What do you mean?" asked Dad.

"Well, I've noticed he's always driving that train," Grady went on. "Him or that skinny elf Carole. What happens if they're both sick or something?"

"Ah!" said Dad, giving me a wink. "Think they might need some help?"

Grady stared toward the door. "Maybe. If it pays."

"You're not old enough to drive," I interrupted.

"Anybody can drive a toy train," said Grady. He grinned. "All you need is half a brain."

That did it. All my elf composure went out the window. "If you wanted a job, why didn't you just ask like a normal person?" I shouted. "Why did you have to sneak around all week, bothering everyone?"

"*Bothering* everyone?" Grady looked at

me like I was the stupidest person alive. "Tinker Bell, haven't you ever heard of *connections*?"

Dad started hooting. He laughed so hard his eyes watered. "Listen," he said when he finally calmed down. "I'll talk to Joanne and see what she says, okay?"

"Yeah, that'd be good," said Grady, shifting from one foot to the other. "I can start anytime. Today, in fact." He shoved his hands into his jacket pockets again. "So I guess I'll see you guys around."

Dad waved his gloved white hand. "Anything else?"

"Not right now," said Grady, hurriedly slipping out the door.

I was just about to tell Dad I thought it was a bad idea to hire juvenile delinquents when the door opened again. "Come on in, folks," said Dad. "Ho, ho, ho!"

I must have the worst luck in the world.

"Megan!" said my best friend. "What are *you* doing here?"

It was Jennifer—you know, the one with the big mouth—standing at a dead stop in the doorway.

"Uh . . ."

"Move," said Jennifer's little brother Sam, pushing her legs. "You're blocking the way."

"Ho, ho, ho. Merry Christmas, kids," said Dad.

Jennifer's eyes opened wide. "Mr. Gallagher?" she said. "Is that you in there?"

"No, no, no. I'm Santa," said Dad.

Jennifer crossed the room to get a closer look. "Sam! It's Mr. Gallagher and Megan. Megan, I don't *believe* this."

"Me, neither," I muttered.

"Come tell Santa what you'd like," said Dad, patting his lap.

"Why is Mr. Gallagher dressed like Santa?" asked Sam.

"Come on up and tell me what you'd like for Christmas, Sam," Dad tried again.

"Why should I tell Mr. Gallagher?" Sam asked Jennifer.

"Just do it, would you?" I said through clenched teeth.

Jennifer was still shaking her head in amazement. "You're too much, Megan. You know that?"

"Do you want your picture taken?" I said. I stomped over to the camera, causing my tights to start their usual downward slide.

Jennifer squealed. "*You're* the one who takes our picture? Sam, look! Meggie's taking our picture!"

38

Sam was finally sitting on Dad's lap, giving him his list. "Will you make sure Santa gets the message, Mr. Gallagher?" he kept asking.

"Ready?" I shouted. I took the picture as quickly as I could, even though I could see Jennifer needed to comb her hair.

"Ho, ho, ho," said Dad, sliding Sam off his lap. "You have a very merry Christmas, you hear? Sparkle, how about a smile for the kids? They came all this way to see Santa Claus!"

Jennifer ran over to me. "Sparkle? Oh, that's so cute! Why didn't you tell me you were playing an elf? You're so lucky!"

I lowered my voice. "Store policy. Our identities are secret."

"Oh," Jennifer whispered. "No wonder."

I pulled the picture out of the camera. "Do you swear on a stack of Bibles you won't tell anyone what you saw today?"

"Sure . . ."

"Good." I handed Jennifer the picture and steered her toward the door before she could notice her hair was messed up and demand a retake.

"Good-bye, Mr. Gallagher," said Sam.

I pulled the door closed after them and took a deep breath. "Dad," I said. "I quit."

Chapter Four

Dad stared at me. "You what?"

Seeing his face, my voice turned all wobbly. "I said, I quit. I don't want to be an elf anymore."

"Why not?" asked Dad, looking truly surprised.

"Because it's embarrassing." I was pretty sure Jennifer wouldn't say anything, especially since she was my best friend, but what if . . . I shuddered . . . anyone else from Carlton Middle School showed up?

Dad's shoulders slumped. "But I thought you were enjoying yourself. Weren't you having fun? You *looked* like you were having fun."

"Dad," I said. "*You're* the one who likes this kind of make-believe, not me."

He was quiet for a long time. "Well, I certainly don't want to force you into anything." He paused. "Are you upset about Grady asking for a job?"

"Sort of. . . . He's not exactly Santa Land material."

"Honey, a cheerful attitude goes a long way around here. Besides, he seems like a perfectly nice kid."

I made a face. "You say that about everyone."

"I do?"

We were interrupted by a knock at the door.

"Ready for a break?" said Elf Marge. "Room two is clear right now."

Dad turned to me. "What if I take you to the Tea Room for lunch and we talk some more?"

I really wasn't in the mood for a "talk," but I guess I'd asked for it. "Okay," I said with a loud enough sigh so he'd know I wasn't thrilled about the date.

Sneaking out of the Santa rooms can be tricky since you can't have all those kids see Santa leave and not return. If it's just a break a Santa is taking, there's a second door in Santa room two that leads out to the back of the sixth floor.

If it's the end of a Santa's shift, though,

he's supposed to walk through the line out front before heading for the dressing room. "Be back in a minute, kids," the Santa says. "I've got to feed my reindeer." Two minutes later, his replacement walks back through the crowd saying, "Hi, kids! I was out feeding my reindeer."

I poked my head into the hallway and signaled to the elf at the end to keep any kids from coming down. "All clear," I said, scooting Dad into room two.

"Sparkle, honey, I'll meet you in the Tea Room in about twenty minutes, okay?"

"Okay," I said, heading for the elf dressing room. I couldn't wait to get rid of my costume.

Behind me, I heard Dad call, "Joanne! Got a minute? I want to ask you something."

My stomach tightened. Good thing I quit. Thinking about Grady as a future employee was enough to make a person question America's future.

Back in the dressing room, it only took a minute for me to change back into my jeans. I balled up my hat and stuffed it for the last time into the back of my locker. I stared at the clock. All the makeup and padding Dad had to take off meant he needed a while to change. To kill some time, I went down to five to visit Oswald.

Oswald is a giant stuffed bear. He sits behind a glass window in a metal booth by the escalator and talks to the kids walking past.

If you want to have a conversation with him, you go up to the window part and talk through this round cutout hole. Inside the booth, in back of Oswald, a real person is hiding behind two long curtains. The person peeps out from between the curtains and moves Oswald's mouth up and down with metal tongs to make it seem like he can really talk. Sort of like the wizard did in *The Wizard of Oz*.

As I walked up, Oswald was doing his routine for a little boy. "Hi," he was saying. "What's your name?"

"Brandon," the little boy whispered.

"You been up to the sixth floor yet to visit Santy Claus?"

Brandon nodded his head.

"Go-o-o-d," said Oswald, dragging the word out. "How 'bout the Story Lady?"

Brandon's head moved slowly back and forth. The Oswald experience tends to freak little kids out to a point of speechlessness.

"Go on over and hear a story then," said Oswald. "And when you're finished you can decorate a Christmas cookie at our cookie table."

Brandon nodded obediently.

"Bye now," said Oswald. "You have a merry Christmas, you hear?"

Brandon's parents thanked Oswald and led their freaked-out kid toward the Story Lady's house.

I stepped on over. "Hi, Megan," said Oswald.

"Hi." This Oswald is really Mr. Thomas, who works the rest of the year on the loading dock. The other Oswald is Mr. Washington from shipping. That Oswald sings Christmas carols on request.

"You helping your dad out today?"

"I was."

"Busy up there?"

"Yeah." I had kind of been hoping Mr. Washington was on duty. I wanted to hear his soul version of "Jingle Bell Rock." It always cheers me up.

I stared out at the crowd of shoppers. The store was jammed today. Then, across the aisle in the linen department, something caught my attention.

"What're you looking at?" said Oswald.

I strained forward. It was that creep Grady, inching his way around one of the pillars.

"Someone I know," I said. Grady had stopped and was peeking around the pillar like a cowboy about to be shot in a movie Western. What *was* he doing? Shoplifting? I watched as he dropped to all fours and started crawling past the bath towels.

"Gotta go now," I told Oswald. Quickly I made my way toward Linens, being careful not to let Grady see me through the crowd. By now he'd stood up again and was slithering toward the rug department. I followed steadily behind.

Suddenly he stopped and spun around.

"Boo!" he screamed at me.

"Eeeeek!" I screamed back, knocking into a display of rug shampoo.

"Ha, ha, ha," said Grady. He clutched his sides and laughed his beady little head off. "Gotcha, didn't I?"

I realized people were staring and quickly composed myself. "Did not."

"Did too." He did a little dance around my feet. "You were following me."

"So? You were acting weird. Why were you sneaking around?" I noticed he was holding a small T. D. Hocker's shopping bag with the receipt stapled to the top. I guess he wasn't shoplifting.

Grady ignored my question. "Listen," he said. "I'm sorry if I made you mad today."

I straightened a few of the shampoo bottles and sniffed. "Any normal person would have just applied for the job."

"Hey!" he said. "Give me a break, okay? It's not like there are thousands of positions around here." He paused. "Especially for a guy like me."

He had a point. Who would want to hire a strange kid who never looked anyone in the eye? Maybe getting on everyone's good side first wasn't such a bad idea.

Another thought occurred to me. "How'd you know where to find my dad every day?"

Grady shuffled his feet. "Easy. I checked the schedule next to the dressing room."

"Oh," I said, trying not to look impressed. "So who gave you permission to go back into the employees-only section?"

Now Grady looked like he was starting to get mad. "Nobody, okay? I helped myself."

I folded my arms. "That's not allowed."

"Aw, give me a break," said Grady. Desperation was starting to creep into his voice. "I need that job, okay?" Now his voice grew softer, almost pleading. "Don't mess it up for me. Please? It's important."

I don't know what happened. But suddenly he looked so sorrowful standing there that something came over me. Maybe it was the Christmas spirit sneaking up.

"Okay," I said. "But you'd better not do anything else against the rules because I'm going to be watching you. And if I see anything funny, I'm telling."

As soon as the words were out of my mouth, I wanted to kick myself. What had I said? Now I had to *keep* my dumb elf job! "Oh brother," I blurted. "Now look what you made me do!"

"What?" asked Grady, thoroughly confused.

"I have to go," I said, bolting off.

I rushed back up to six, cursing my bad luck the whole way. I found Dad waiting on a sofa in the Tea Room, anxiously stirring his coffee. "There you are!" he said. "I was beginning to think you'd run off to the North Pole with Rudolph."

"Sorry," I said, still panting from my run up the escalator. "I wasn't paying attention to the time." I swallowed. "I've been thinking. Maybe I won't quit after all."

Dad looked as surprised as I felt.

"Maybe I overreacted," I went on. "The

only time it's really embarrassing to be an elf is when I know the people."

"Which rarely happens," said Dad. "Today was a fluke."

"A fluke," I repeated. I hoped he was right, because I was about to sacrifice my dignity in order to make sure the law was upheld.

Dad stared at me sternly. "What about Grady? I thought you were upset about his asking for a job."

I crossed my fingers. "Oh, I guess he deserves to work if he wants to. Did he get the job?"

Dad reached out to squeeze my other hand. "I spoke to Joanne about him. I know you think I'm too soft on people, Meggie, but he's a nice kid. He could use a chance."

"I know," I said reluctantly.

Dad was still holding my hand, which was starting to get a little embarrassing. "I'm glad you're going to stick around," he said. "I like it when you help me out. It's special for me."

"Me, too," I said, feeling guilty. Okay, so my motives weren't entirely honest. True, I wanted to spend time with Dad, but I also had an obligation now to make sure Grady was a model employee. I have to admit I was curious, too. Why did Grady sound so desperate? It was only a dumb job. Did he need the money to help his family out? And another thing, he still hadn't told me why he had been sneaking on all fours across the showroom floor.

"You know those scuba lessons you were interested in?" said Dad, interrupting my thoughts. "I mentioned them to Mom."

"You did?" The guilt factor intensified.

"Maybe you can give Santa a list of the equipment you need."

I was tempted to do it right then, but my better judgment told me to wait.

The Tea Room hostess came over. "Your table's ready, Ed."

We navigated our way across the room, past groups of hungry shoppers surrounded by their purchases.

"Menu?" asked the waitress as I slid into my chair.

"Thanks." I wasn't sure how I had suddenly ended up on Grady's side, but it didn't feel *that* wrong to be there. With school vacation starting at the end of the week, Dad would be needing some extra help—giving me the chance to find out what was going on.

"Is something wrong?" asked Dad.

"No," I said, opening up the menu. I crossed my fingers one more time. "At least I hope not."

Chapter Five

Would you believe "Casey Jones" Watkins started the very next day? Dad must've done *some* selling job, because Grady hadn't even had time to fill out an application. In fact, he was already at the controls when we reported for duty at noon. "He's doing fine," Joanne said as we stood together by the train entrance. "A little heavy on the pedal sometimes, but other than that . . ."

Just then Grady rounded the corner, his body hunched over the controls like a jockey on a racehorse. When he saw us, he broke into a grin and began tooting the horn and waving his striped engineer's cap. "Yo, Ed! How do I look?"

"Good," Dad shouted back. "Two hands on the wheel, son." Grady nodded and gunned the engine.

"Show-off," I said under my breath. I checked out the line; it stretched nearly to the elevators even though we'd just opened up.

"Shall we get started?" asked Dad. We were scheduled for twelve thirty to five thirty, a short day. Dad needed a rest, and I'd promised Mom I'd help her clean the house before Sarah came home for vacation.

I forgot to mention about Sarah. She called last night. "I'm getting a ride Monday with someone heading our direction," she said. "A guy named Kink."

"Kink?" said Mom.

"As in kinky?" I said, listening in on the extension.

"Megan, hang up the phone," said Mom. "When are you getting in, honey?"

"Around six," said Sarah.

"Is Kink staying for dinner?" Mom asked.

"What are we having?" asked Sarah.

"Tuna fish," I said. "On toast." Sarah hates tuna fish. It makes her break out in a rash.

"Megan! Hang up the phone."

"Hi, Meggie," said Sarah, laughing. "Dad said you've got elf duty this year."

"It was an accident."

Sarah laughed even harder. She's another

one of those people who thinks I'm funny.

"Megan," interrupted Mom. "Don't you have homework?"

"I did it already."

"Well, maybe you can lick stamps for me." We must send five hundred Christmas cards a year. Everyone we ever met gets one . . . the neighbors, the dry cleaner, the paper girl. We even send a card to this couple, Tom and Ida. My parents met them on their honeymoon and never saw them again.

I could feel my tongue crinkle up. "Do I have to?"

"Megan . . ."

"Never mind." I hung up the phone. Sometimes I wonder whether I was secretly adopted.

When I got home from school Monday afternoon, Mom was already in the kitchen, whipping up Sarah's favorite dinner, baked ham with mashed potatoes and applesauce.

"Did I tell you I've decided to become a vegetarian?" I said, throwing my coat on a chair.

"Wait until tomorrow," said Mom, shoving another clove into the ham.

I pushed aside some fruitcake tins and

pulled myself up to sit on the kitchen table. "Poor little pig."

"How was school?" asked Mom.

"Okay." Other than the fact that I got to spy on Trevor every day in the lunchroom (today he was eating a peanut butter and jelly sandwich), I couldn't wait for vacation. Every time I'd seen Jennifer lately, she'd winked at me. And today before history I caught her whispering something to Heather McQueen while I was putting my notebook away.

Mom looked at me. "If you're not doing anything right now, Megan, you can set the table. The snowflake place mats are in the second drawer. Dad's due home any minute," she added.

"Ho, ho, ho. I'm h-o-o-me!" yelled Dad from the front door, right on cue. "Sur-prise!"

"Now what can that mean?" asked Mom.

"You must be Anne!" said Grady, popping his head into the kitchen.

"Oh no!" I groaned. "Not you again!"

"Hey," said Grady, throwing out his arms. "I was invited, okay?"

"Hope it's all right to add one more person tonight, Anne," said Dad, casting me the evil eye as he followed Grady into the room. "This is Grady Watkins, train engineer."

"I've heard a lot about you," said Mom, smiling at Grady just like the mother on *Lassie*. "Can I fix you an eggnog?"

While I looked for another place mat, Grady cased the room. "Yeah, sure. Thanks." His eyes came to rest on a pair of angel salt and pepper shakers. "Very nice house. Very nice."

Mom's face lit up. "Why, thank you!" She handed Grady his eggnog. "Would you like a tour?" She turned to me. "Megan?"

"I've seen it aleady."

Grady started to laugh.

"Megan!" said Mom. "I meant . . ."

"Oh." I lifted my arm. "This is the kitchen," I pointed. "In there is the living room. Upstairs are the bedrooms." I wasn't about to show Grady Mom and Dad's mistletoe bedspread. "Want to play a video game?"

"Sure."

Relieved, I led the way to the family room.

"Geez. You've got more decorations than Hocker's," said Grady, running his fingers over one of Mom's needlepoint light-switch covers.

I flipped on the TV and sat down on the couch. "You can go first."

Grady was still busy sight-seeing.

"Your turn," I repeated loudly. Now you see why I never invite anyone over after December first.

"I heard your sister's coming home tonight," said Grady, finally picking up the control pad. He immediately racked up a jillion points.

"What about it?" I answered.

"What's she like?"

I tried to picture Sarah in my mind. It had been a few months since I'd seen her. "Well . . . she looks like Mom, she acts like Dad, and every day she wears a different Christmas pin on her outfit."

Grady burst out laughing, then suddenly threw down the control pad. "See there? You made me mess up."

"About time," I said, picking up the pad. "So what about you? Do *you* have any brothers or sisters?"

He pursed his lips together. "No."

"You mean you're an only child?" Somehow he didn't seem the type.

Grady thumped his hands on the sofa. "C'mon, will ya? It's your turn."

"What do your parents do?"

"They work. Now take your turn, okay?"

Something wasn't right, but I could see I

wasn't going to get anything else out of him just then.

I had barely started playing when I heard Dad calling that Sarah had arrived.

"Let's go," said Grady, hopping off the couch.

I took my time finishing my turn. In the front hall, Sarah was making her usual commotion greeting everyone. "Meggie!" she cried when I finally came in. She threw her arms around me. "How's my baby sister? God, you grew!"

Behind Sarah hovered a mysterious-looking guy with a thick beard and a ruby in one ear.

"Thanks," I said to Sarah while trying to untangle myself from her squeeze. I leaned back to check her out. "What happened to your hair?"

Sarah relaxed her grasp. "I permed it. Do you like it?"

To be honest, she reminded me of Peppy, our neighbor's poodle.

She tugged on her bangs. "The front needs to grow out some."

"Yeah." On her sweatshirt I spotted one of her Christmas pins. "The rest of you hasn't changed."

"Oh, Meggie, I love you."

I squinched my face and braced myself for another squeeze.

"Has everyone met?" asked Dad. Grady had evaporated into the wings, and now Dad pulled him forward into the spotlight. "This is Grady—another one of Santa's fine helpers. I noticed him hanging around the elevators after work and thought he looked hungry."

Grady nodded uncomfortably.

"And this is Kink," said Sarah. "He's an art major."

"This house is really something," said Kink.

"Thanks," said Mom. "I hope you're staying for dinner."

"I never refuse food," he said.

Once the introductions were finished, everyone reassembled in the dining room, but not before we listened to Sarah ooh and ah her way past every single decoration in her path. "Look! The elf figurines! And here's my snowman music box. And my stocking! Oh, you even have the holly bowls with the candy canes."

I rolled my eyes. Kink smiled at me.

In the dining room, Mom flew around the table telling people where to sit. I eased myself over near Kink. "Megan?" said Mom, pointing to the chair beside Grady.

I sighed and plopped into my assigned seat. Why is it that grown-ups lump kids together just because they're in the same age category?

Across the table, Sarah was monopolizing the conversation, going on and on about how nice it was to be home and how great everything looked and blah blah blah blah blah.

I peeked at Grady and was surprised to see he didn't look too good. His face was paler than usual, and his hands were clasped tightly in his lap. I realized he hadn't said a word since Sarah's arrival.

"Are you okay?" I whispered. He looked like he was about to barf.

"Sure I am," said Grady stiffly. "Why wouldn't I be?"

Maybe Sarah had overwhelmed him. Or maybe it was all of us. I put my napkin on my lap. Grady put his on his lap.

Mom called me into the kitchen to help. I guess now that Sarah's in college, she's considered a guest.

I helped Mom deliver the soups. "I hope everyone likes cream of tomato," she said, sailing into the dining room with the green tureen.

"How colorful," said Kink.

One thing I forgot to mention. Mom is into food themes—especially at holiday time. On St. Patrick's Day, we have green pancakes. On Valentine's Day, we have only red foods (ham, tomatoes, Jell-O, etc.). I hadn't realized it, but this was going to be another of Mom's red-and-green dinners.

I sat back down and removed the parsley from my soup. Grady did the same. Slowly, I picked up my spoon and took a first taste, allowing time for Grady to copy me.

At the head of the table, Dad beamed. "Is everybody happy?"

"This is great," said Kink, polishing off his parsley.

Good thing he was an artist. Wait until he saw the green mashed potatoes and pink applesauce.

Chapter Six

I guess you could say Sarah's welcome-home dinner was a success. Grady and Kink had seconds and thirds, Sarah eventually let the rest of us contribute to the conversation, and for once, Dad didn't suggest that we move into the living room after dinner to sing Christmas carols.

One weird thing happened, though. While we were eating dessert (pink peppermint ice cream with green mint sauce and Christmas cookies), Grady asked Kink, "Would you mind giving me a ride back downtown?"

"I'll be happy to take you home, son," Dad interrupted.

"No, no," said Grady, waving his hands. "Forget about it, Ed."

"I don't mind, Mr. Gallagher," said Kink. "I wanted to see the downtown anyway."

I could see Dad's feelings were kind of hurt. "Well . . . whatever."

Grady shifted around in his chair. "Uh, I need to be back before nine, okay?" He could see that the rest of us were looking at him. "Busy day tomorrow, right?"

Kink nodded agreeably. "Sure, man. Whatever."

Grady sighed and sat back.

"What street are you on?" asked Mom politely.

"A street downtown," said Grady. "You probably never heard of it."

"Try me," said Mom, who could draw a map of downtown blindfolded if she wanted to.

"No, no," said Grady. "Really."

Mom dropped the subject.

That night I got to thinking. It seemed obvious that Grady was keeping something from the rest of us. I tiptoed into Sarah's room.

"Hi," she said. Her stuff was all over the place. "Do you know what happened to my Trent Wilson poster?"

I swallowed. "You mean the one that was on the wall?"

She nodded.

"Oh. I think it might be in my room."

"That's *my* poster, Megan."

"Okay," I sighed. "I'll return it." I moved a mountain of dirty laundry aside and sat down on the bed. "When do you start at Hocker's?"

"Tomorrow." She tossed me a sweatshirt with Delta spelled out across the front. "Want it? It shrank."

"Sure! Thanks." I watched as she carefully arranged everything back onto her dresser the way it had always been. "I was wondering . . . You know that guy Grady who was here for dinner tonight?"

"What about him?"

I told Sarah what I knew, leaving out the part about him slinking across the fifth floor the other day. I didn't want her to get the wrong impression.

When I finished, she shrugged and said, "So what's your point, Meggie?"

"I think he's up to something, don't you?"

Sarah laughed. "Oh, Meggie. You've always had such a wild imagination. Where do you come up with these ideas?"

"They're not ideas!" I said indignantly. "They're real." See what I mean about Sarah? She's just like Dad. People are innocent until proven guilty.

"Okay, okay," she said sweetly. "They're real, Meggie." Now she was busy making sure all her cologne bottles faced forward.

I waited a minute and then asked, "So, could you keep an eye on him this week?"

"Sure," she said. "If I see him." She turned to me. "Can you keep a secret?"

It sort of bothered me that she didn't take my request seriously. "I guess."

From her dresser drawer, Sarah pulled out something wrapped in tissue paper. "I got this for Mom and Dad at an antique store."

I watched her carefully unwind the object from the paper. "Look. It's a Christmas cuckoo clock," she said. "Isn't it adorable? Instead of a cuckoo, a Santa comes out every hour and says, 'Ho, ho, ho.' "

"Mmmm," I said, politely. "A Christmas decoration!"

Sarah laughed. "You're such a comedian. Here." She handed me a strand of tiny colored Christmas lights. "Want to help me put these around my dresser mirror? I had them up in my dorm room and they looked great."

"Sure," I answered. "Whatever." The comedian speaks.

The next evening was *Amahl*. I'd been looking forward to it all week, so I was ready way before Jennifer's mother came to pick me up. "Wow! You look different," said Jennifer as I climbed into the car. "Where'd you get that leather skirt?"

"Sarah's closet," I said, pulling my coat closer in case Sarah was looking out the window. "I don't think she's worn it yet." I leaned over. "How about my perfume? Does it stink too much?"

Jennifer sniffed deeply. "It'll wear off by the time we get there." She squinted her eyes. "You have on lip gloss, too?"

"My lips are chapped," I said, lying. I didn't want to seem too overdone.

Jennifer giggled. "You're too much, Megan." She paused. "How's Santa?"

I looked around the car. "Santa? Santa who?"

"Sorry, sorry," she said. "I forgot."

For the rest of the ride, we talked about Trevor. Our relationship hadn't progressed much. Maybe tonight would be different. Finally, we pulled into the St. Luke's parking lot.

"I'll pick you girls up here after the performance, all right?" said Mrs. Parkes.

"Okay," said Jennifer. "Thanks, Mom."

We made our way inside, Jennifer taking regular steps and me taking tiny ones, in my tight skirt. "Slow down," I whispered. "I can't keep up."

The church was beautiful. Each pew was lined with evergreen roping, and jillions of red poinsettias dotted the center stage area, which had been made up to look like a poor shepherd's hut.

We got our programs and walked down the center aisle to the very front row. "You take the aisle seat," said Jennifer, sliding around me. "Higher visibility."

"Oh," I said. "Thanks." I never would have thought of that. I twisted around. We were practically the first ones there. "Now what?"

"Now we wait," said Jennifer, opening her program. As she read, I watched for Trevor and practiced keeping my legs together. Finally, the church was full, and the organ began to play its opening song. I clutched Jennifer's arm.

"There he is!" I gasped. Trevor entered on the far side of the room. He was dressed in rags, with his hair messed up as if he'd forgotten to comb it. Slowly, painfully, he hopped on one crutch across the stage. "Poor Trevor," I whispered to Jennifer. I started feeling sorry for him, the cutest boy in school, looking like that in front of all those people.

And then he began to sing. Forget everything I just said. Trevor Harris has a voice as clear and pure as an angel's. I sat with my mouth half open, listening to that voice curl up into the rafters like the smoke from a stick of burning incense.

Jennifer leaned over. "So what do you think?"

"I think it was worth the five dollars," I whispered back. "Even if he doesn't notice me."

Trevor hobbled into his hut, where he and his mother sang a song about being too poor to buy food.

They had barely fallen asleep when the Three Kings, the ones of Orient Are, arrived looking for a place to spend the night. Amahl got the door, and naturally his mother didn't believe him when he told her who was there. Was she surprised! She was so nervous and excited to have three kings as guests that she invited all the other peasants to come meet them and bring food.

Which is why the goat showed up.

I don't know how these things happen to me. There I was, minding my own business, listening rapturously to Trevor, when the peasant chorus came in and positioned itself directly beside me.

"Look!" said Jennifer, nudging my arm. "A real goat!" The goat was standing with one of the peasants a few feet away, sniffing on some evergreen roping. "Isn't it cute?"

Suddenly the goat gave a lurch with its neck, pulling its rope out of the peasant's hand. "Oh no!" I gasped as it bolted off.

The goat wandered to the right, over to the baptismal fountain, and tried to get a drink. The audience began to laugh. Then the peasant in charge of the goat tried to sneak over and corner it by the organ, but that just made it run back onto the middle of the stage. The peasant looked disgusted. "Poor guy," Jennifer whispered.

The rest of the peasant chorus headed off. The goatherd made one more attempt to grab his goat. No luck. It looked as if Trevor, his mother, and the Three Kings were going to have to deal with it.

Onstage, the goat nibbled on an ivy plant, then poked around a hay bale for a while. I sort of hoped it would keep quiet, since it was stealing the show from Trevor. That's when it decided to wander back into the audience.

Maybe it was Sarah's perfume that attracted the goat to me, I'm not sure. All I know is that I was not in any way trying to lure the goat when, out of the blue, it found me. "Nice goat," I said as quietly as possible. It moved a little closer, its gummy nose twitching back and forth. I gave it a gentle shove. "Go find the peasants, okay?" I whispered. "Go on."

The goat braced its body against my hand. Jennifer started to giggle, which didn't help the situation.

"Go *away*." I felt a tug, which I tried ignoring. Then another. That's when I looked down at my lap and saw what that disgusting little goat was up to. "Oh my God," I gasped. "He's chewing on my leather skirt!"

I pushed the goat as hard as I could, sending him flying. Was it *my* fault Trevor was standing three feet away, on one feeble crutch, which now had a goat hurtling toward it?

"*Aaaeee!*" screamed Trevor. They crashed to the floor—goat, crutch, and boy in one big tangle. And then Trevor looked up, right at me. So I did the only thing I could think to do in such a moment. I waved.

Afterward, on the way home, Jennifer said to me, "Well, look at it this way. At least he won't ever forget you."

"Great," I said miserably. "And neither will Sarah when she finds tooth marks on her new skirt."

"How was the performance, girls?" interrupted Mrs. Parkes.

Jennifer started laughing. "You should have seen what happened to Megan," she said, going over the gory details again.

When Jennifer finished, Mrs. Parkes said, "You're lucky Trevor wasn't hurt and the show could go on." I could tell she was being polite and trying not to laugh.

I looked down at Sarah's chewed-up skirt and winced. Yep, I thought, that's me. Megan Gallagher. The luckiest person in the world.

Chapter Seven

Sarah was really mad about the skirt. At first, I tried telling her the tooth marks came from my coat zipper, but she wouldn't buy it. "You should know better than to go poking through my things without asking," she said with a sniff. "I was saving that skirt for New Year's Eve." She eyed me up and down. "Besides, you're much too young to be wearing leather. You'd have looked better in your green velvet jumper."

"Euuuuu. Yuck," I said, which Sarah thought was totally hilarious.

The worst part of the whole thing, though, was that Mom made me pay for the skirt out of my savings account. Fifty big ones. Between that and buying Christmas gifts, I was now completely broke. It would probably be a million years before I could ever save that much money again.

As for Trevor, I avoided him until Friday, when our Christmas vacation started. Maybe by January he'd be ready to hear my explanation.

Besides, strange things were happening on the Grady front that demanded my attention. For one thing, Sarah came through and reported that Grady came into the Gourmet Market every single day for a jumbo can of popcorn. "I give him the employee discount," she said. "Don't you think he'll get cavities eating all that sticky popcorn?"

"I don't think he's the kind of person who worries about cavities, Sarah."

"Everyone should worry about cavities," she said.

I sighed.

Then a day or two later Sarah said, "I had the weirdest conversation with Grady today."

"What about?"

"I started asking him about his family. He got very defensive and said that it was none of my business. Then I made the mistake of asking him where he lived, and he wouldn't tell me."

"See what I mean?" I said. "Why wouldn't he tell you where he lived? Do you think he's embarrassed?"

Sarah shrugged. "I don't know. Some people are funny. They like to keep things to themselves."

I knew it was none of my business, and I knew it was rude to snoop, but now I was really curious. Nosy Megan Gallagher. I couldn't help myself. Besides, what if something was really wrong? What if he needed help?

The next night, Wednesday, it happened that Sarah had to go pick Dad up, since she'd taken the car home earlier.

"Can I come?" I asked.

"Sure," she said. I knew she was only doing it to be polite. Things were still a little strained between us because of the skirt. I wanted to check on Grady, though. Find out what he was up to.

Downtown, the store was in its usual holiday jam. "Don't you just *love* this?" said Sarah, cheerfully stepping onto the main floor. We started to wrestle our way across the room. "Stay close, Meggie. I don't want to lose you." Halfway there, Sarah stopped and flung out her arms. "Ahhh." She gave a happy wave to a friend of hers in Cosmetics. "Yoo-hoo. Michelle!"

Just then I got slammed in the side by a shopping bag. "Ow!"

"Oh no! Are you okay?" asked Sarah.

I rubbed my hip and nodded. "Can I meet you and Dad in the Tea Room? I have some shopping to do."

She smiled at me like I was a seven year old. "I guess it's okay for you to go off by yourself. Just be careful, okay, sweetie?"

My eyes narrowed. "My name is Megan, not sweetie."

"You don't need to overreact, Megan."

"And *you* don't need to treat me like a baby, Sarah."

She looked insulted. "I don't!"

"Yes, you do. You always do. It's like I have three parents."

She did exactly what I expected, which was laugh.

"See you in a few minutes," I said, pushing past her. I didn't really have any strategy for finding Grady, and now that I was mad at Sarah I didn't have any patience, either.

I headed up the escalator, in the general direction of Santa Land, stopping only once on two to let a lady wearing a red felt hat decorated with holly blast me with the perfume of the day.

When I got to four, I stepped off, thinking I'd walk around Housewares and cool down for a minute. Instead I ran right into the one person I was hoping to find. "Grady!"

He gave me a friendly nod. "What are you doing here?"

"Um . . . shopping!" I pivoted to my right. Then my left. "Mom wanted some new wine glasses. I think they're over here."

"No, they're over there," said Grady. "With the wedding junk. C'mon. I'll show you." He skirted around a holiday display of video games and zigzagged his way to the back of the floor.

"You sure know your way around," I said, puffing to keep up. "How's your job?"

"The money's decent."

"What're you going to *do* with the money?"

"I'm saving it."

"For what?"

Grady stopped, then grinned. "None of your business, nosy." I could feel my cheeks burn. "C'mere," said Grady. "I want to show you something." He led me over to an area filled with silver and crystal wedding gifts: wine decanter sets, lacy-looking glasses, engraved pitchers, and fancy ice buckets. Then he pointed to a prominently placed shelf. "These are glass animal sculptures. There's a whale, a polar bear, a seal, and a fish."

"Wow," I said.

Grady shook his head. "Beautiful, huh? Made from a single piece of blown glass. I come here a lot to admire them. Someday I'm gonna own one." He carefully picked up the polar bear and handed it to me. "This guy's my favorite. Feel how solid he is? What do you think he costs?"

"I don't know."

He looked around and lowered his voice. "Would you believe a hundred dollars?"

"You're kidding." I could feel my palm, the one currently worth one hundred dollars, begin to perspire.

His face broke out in a grin. "Ya, ya, just kidding."

"Grady!" I gave him a shove, accidentally causing that same perspiring palm to lose its grip. With a dull clunk, the polar bear dropped to the floor. "Uh-oh." The bear's head, neatly severed, rolled under the shelf.

Grady went pale. Really pale. "Megan!" He glanced around. "I was kidding about that bear being worth one hundred dollars, because he's *really* worth two hundred dollars."

Now it was my turn to feel sick.

"Put it back on the shelf and walk away," said Grady.

"What!"

"Listen, George Washington. You got two hundred dollars lying around?"

I bent over stiffly.

"Hurry," whispered Grady. "Someone's coming."

I placed the headless bear back on the display shelf. "What if someone saw?"

"They didn't. Now let's get out of here," said Grady. We headed to the escalators and didn't stop or look back until we reached the Tea Room.

"There you are!" said Sarah. She and Dad were perched expectantly on the sofa.

"Hi, Sarah. Hi, Dad."

Dad gave us his holiday grin. "Well! What have you two been up to?"

I swallowed. "Nothing." Grady's normally darting eyes were fixed on the floor.

"Ready to go?" asked Dad.

"Uh, sure."

"When are you working again?" Grady asked me.

"Saturday," I answered.

"Okay," said Grady. "Take it easy."

I tried not to think about the headless polar bear or Grady for the rest of the week. But a few times late at night I felt guilty about breaking the bear and putting it back without saying anything. Okay, not *that* guilty, since I knew I'd never have enough money to pay for it, but guilty enough that by Saturday I was not especially looking forward to seeing Grady *or* Hocker's.

There I was, though, Saturday morning at nine, standing in the elf dressing room, getting suited up for the day. I checked the clock. Dad and I were scheduled for room three from nine thirty to six thirty, with an hour and a half break from one thirty to three. I'd been warned that this was to be the busiest weekend of the season.

I finished dressing and made my way through the back hall and over to the time clock, where Dad and I had arranged to meet. I glanced up at the schedule. Oh great. Grady's break was scheduled the same time as mine. One part of me still wanted to find out why he was so mysterious, but the other part just wanted to avoid him.

"Ho, ho, ho," said Dad, coming up behind me.

I spun around. "Oh, hi, Da—Santa."

"Everything okay?"

"I was just thinking about something, that's all."

"Well, save your thinking for our Gingerbread House today," said Dad, grabbing my hand. "You're going to need it."

Dad wasn't kidding when he said this was the busiest day of the season. Our morning was completely crazy. It seemed as if every kid we saw that day asked either for a Baby Wet Wet or a Power Shield. Then, just when I thought I'd heard every possible request, a kid came in and asked for his dad back.

Dad got real quiet. So did the kid's mom. Then Dad sort of "ummed" for a few seconds. Finally he said, "Santa can do a lot of things, Justin, but he can't do everything."

Justin kind of picked at Dad's beard. "I know that." He was probably about five years old.

"Tell Santa what toys you want," said the mother, trying to change the subject.

Justin named a few of the popular ones, but I could tell he was still thinking about his dad.

When he finished, Dad said, "Santa loves you, buddy, you know that?"

"Yep."

"How about a hug?"

Justin reached his arms up around Dad's neck and squeezed.

"See you next year, okay, pal?"

"Okay," said Justin. He slid off Dad's lap. "We might be moving to Florida."

"That's okay," said Dad. "I'll find you."

Justin smiled.

After Justin left, Dad said to me, "How you doing, Meggie?"

To tell you the truth, I wasn't doing that great. I felt terrible for that kid, wanting his dad so much he asked Santa for him. "Does that happen very often?"

"More than it should." Dad pulled me close. "Believe me, it breaks my heart to see it. But that's why I'm here, honey, for kids like that."

"But you can't give him what he wants."

"No. But I can let him know he's loved." Dad stood up and unstuck the sweaty Santa suit from his back. "That's what it's all about,

Meggie. Hope. Santa represents the spirit of hope, whether it's wishing for toys or wishing for a dad."

I frowned.

Dad sighed. "Oh, Meggie. Sometimes I wish I could do more."

"I know, Dad."

He suddenly brightened and winked at me. "But hope's a powerful thing, Meggie. Don't underestimate it. And don't underestimate Santa, either."

"What's that supposed to mean?"

"Sometimes Santa can surprise people."

I knew Santa couldn't surprise Justin, but I wondered if he could somehow erase that polar bear incident.

Abruptly Dad glanced at his watch. "Break time. Can you believe it?"

"Already?"

"Want to have lunch together?"

"Um, sorry, Dad. Not today." As soon as I turned him down, I could see he needed company. "Maybe Mrs. Claus can join you. She's on break, too." I gave him a good long hug and then headed to the dressing room. Maybe I *would* try to find Grady.

I changed into my normal clothes and went out to the time clock. Darn. Missed him. I saw Mrs. Claus approaching. "Have you seen Grady?" I asked.

"He said he had some shopping to do," she answered.

"Thanks." I headed down the escalator, hoping to catch up with him.

Halfway to three, I caught sight of the back of his head disappearing around a corner. "Grady!" I called. "Wait up!" He must not have heard me. I followed him, through Ladies' Dresses and into the children's department, where I suddenly stopped. Why was Grady plowing through girls' dresses, size 6X? All I could think was maybe he had a little sister until I remembered he said he was an only child.

Something told me not to reveal myself—not yet. I hid behind a pole and watched. Grady chose a denim skirt and matching vest (not the greatest looking in my opinion, but what kind of taste should I have expected from Grady?) and paid for them with cash. Then I followed him down to the Gourmet Market, where he bought a giant can of popcorn (bubblegum flavor) and a couple of fancy chocolate-chip cookies from Sarah.

After that he went up to four, where he spent a long time in Electronics playing with the computer and video games and snacking on popcorn. Nothing wrong with that, except maybe getting popcorn grease on the computer keyboards. I was beginning to wonder why I was following him when he disappeared. Vanished.

He left Electronics, took the escalator up to five, walked through Rugs, slipped around a dark corner, and *poof!* He was gone. I'm not kidding. It was like something out of *The Twilight Zone.*

I traced his path around the corner. All I saw was a large pile of rugs and an empty desk. No doors. No windows. I walked over and looked under the rug pile. Nothing. I even opened the desk drawers. He simply wasn't there.

One of the salespeople walked over. "May I help you?"

"I don't think so."

The salesman looked at me strangely.

"Did you see a boy wearing black jeans come through here?" I asked.

"No." He folded his arms across his chest. "But I did see you going through my desk."

I choked. "Me? Me? Oh . . . I guess I was . . . I was looking for someone. . . ."

"In my desk?"

I tried smiling.

"Maybe I should call security," said the salesman.

Terror gripped my throat. "For me? But I work here. I'm my father's elf."

The salesman wasn't smiling. "What's your name?"

"Megan. Megan Gallagher. Do you know Ed Gallagher in Ladies' Shoes?"

"Vaguely."

I could see this was getting me nowhere fast. "I think I should be going now."

"I think so, too," said the salesman.

I tore out of there so quick you'd have thought my rear end was on fire. I guess it served me right for being so nosy.

Dad and Mrs. Claus were in the Tea Room, finishing up their apple pies. "This is a surprise," said Dad.

"You're telling me." I gulped a few sips of Dad's ice water.

"You seem rather flushed, Megan," said Mrs. Claus.

"Is anything the matter, Meggie?" asked Dad.

"No. Everything's fine."

"Can I get you some pie?" Dad asked.

At that moment, I looked across the room, and who do you think I saw walking back to Santa Land? "No, thanks," I said, bolting from my chair. "I'm not hungry."

Grady slipped through the waiting crowd toward the back of the store. I noticed his packages were gone.

I found him at the time clock, punching in. "Hi," I said, trying to make it seem like I just *happened* to run into him. "Where've you been?"

"No place," he said. "I was on my break."

I stood there waiting, not sure what to say next.

Grady pulled his engineer's cap out of his back pocket and started for the floor. "Well, gotta get back to work. See you."

"Um . . . Grady?"

He turned around. "Yeah?"

"I . . . I feel bad about breaking that bear and then not telling anyone."

For one instant, he lowered his eyes. "Yeah, me, too. But what can you do? It was an accident, right?" He looked up again. "Well, don't wanna be late. See you later, Tinker Bell."

He swaggered off, cool as can be.

Chapter Eight

For the rest of the afternoon, it was hard to concentrate on kids when I wanted to concentrate on Grady. His mysterious disappearance was driving me crazy. "Are we going home right after work tonight?" I asked Dad at one point.

"I was sort of planning on it," Dad answered. "Why?"

"Well . . . I still have some shopping to do," I said.

"How much time do you need?"

"An hour?"

"I guess we can manage that."

An hour's a lot when you're not getting anywhere. By the time I changed and got back to the front of Santa Land, Grady had already left.

"Shoot," I said to myself. "Shoot, shoot, shoot, shoot, shoot." I searched the sixth floor for any sign of him and, when I couldn't find him, took the escalator down to five.

"Why so blue?" said Oswald as I stepped off. Oswald was Mr. Washington this time. I could tell by his deep voice.

"I'm sort of looking for someone," I said. "The skinny kid who drives the Santa Land train. Know him?"

"Mmmmm," said Oswald.

"What can you tell me about him?"

"Sometimes old Oswald's got mighty sharp eyes."

My heart started speeding. I stood on my tippy toes and leaned toward the glass window. "Have you seen Grady around here?"

"Yes, ma'am. See him all the time."

I caught my breath. "Is he in trouble?"

"No, ma'am," said Oswald. "He's peculiar, that's all." I let out my breath. Oswald hummed a few bars of a tune I didn't recognize.

A couple of kids came up behind me and got in line. "Why? What kind of peculiar?" I asked.

"Hi, kids," said Oswald. "Be with you in a minute." He lowered his voice and spoke to me again. "I've noticed he's always glancing behind himself and taking indirect routes around the room. The oddest thing about him, though, is what he does with his parcels."

"What do you mean?"

"He's like a pack rat or something. For instance, he came down here yesterday with a shopping bag and hid it under that Christmas tree over there. Then a couple of hours later, he came back, took that bag out, and put it and another parcel under those Persians."

I figured he meant the Persian rugs.

Oswald cleared his throat. "Why would anyone be taking his parcels and hiding them in the store?"

I wondered the same thing. I knew Grady had a locker in the employee dressing room, so why would he be stuffing things under rugs on the fifth floor?

Oswald raised his voice. "Okay, who's next? What's your name, young man?"

I stepped aside unwillingly, determined to find out more once Oswald was free again.

"Jamal," said the boy. "The Story Lady told me to ask for 'Jingle Bell Rock.'"

Oswald launched into his famous soul version of the song, attracting a few more kids to the line. I could see this would take a while, so I wandered over to where Grady had vanished earlier and poked around the rugs, feeling for packages. Nothing. I glanced at my watch. Only a half hour left till closing. Already, the crowd of shoppers had started to thin. All across the floor, cash registers were ringing down.

Frustrated, I sat down on a tall pile of rugs and stared at the wall. Then something caught my eye. I noticed a movable panel about three feet above the floor. An extension cord hung down from behind it and was plugged into an outlet. Why would an extension cord be here, especially one leading *inside*?

I walked over and pushed the panel gently. With a quiet creak, it swung open from the bottom.

Something told me to keep going. Quickly I glanced around to make sure no one was watching—especially that rug salesman—then I poked my head inside. I saw a dark space, about four feet wide. On the far side was a built-in steel ladder leading up to what looked like some sort of landing. The extension cord dangled invitingly beside the ladder.

At this point, my heart, which was already beating faster than normal, went into extra innings. That extension cord had to be going somewhere, and I, nosy Megan Gallagher, was going to follow it.

I hopped inside the crawl space, pushed

the panel shut, and began climbing the ladder, rung by rung, quickly reaching the top. The extension cord stretched across an enormous flat surface. I climbed onto it, then reached up and touched the ceiling—which was only about four feet above the floor.

Dust choked my nostrils. The dark made it difficult to see, but by now I was determined. Clinging to the cord, I began to edge forward on my hands and knees. So far, what I was crawling across seemed sturdy enough. As long as my bravery held out, I figured I was okay.

I followed the extension cord around a few more corners, still not sure where I'd end up. I thought I heard voices, but wasn't sure. And then ahead of me, I noticed an eerie light flickering against the far wall.

Still gripping the extension cord, I edged closer. The light and sound seemed to be coming from a TV set, but that wasn't all. As I got nearer my eyes adjusted, and I noticed a couple of spread-out sleeping bags, a small desk light, a big cushion for leaning against, and a familiar container of bubblegum-flavored gourmet popcorn. And beside *that* lay Grady Watkins, stretched out on another sleeping bag, watching a cop show. He glanced up.

"Holy moly!" he said, springing into a crouch. "What are *you* doing here?"

My hand dropped the cord like I'd just been electrocuted. "What are *you* doing here?"

We stared at each other. "What does it look like?" said Grady finally. "I live here."

I swallowed. "In the store? You *live* in the store?" I noticed the TV and the desk lamp still had their price tags. "Since when?"

"Since . . . I don't know. What's it to you?" He nervously balled up a couple of dirty T-shirts and tossed them into a dark corner.

I noticed the size 6X denim outfit, a pink-and-green girl's jacket, and a bottle of perfume beside a roll of wrapping paper and some ribbon. "Where's your family? Your mom and dad?"

He waved his hand. "At *their* house," he answered. His eyes narrowed. "Did anyone see you come up?"

"I'd like to know what's going on," I said firmly.

Grady ignored me. "How did you find me, anyway? Figures *you'd* be the one."

"I want to know why you're living in T. D. Hocker's ceiling," I said, sticking to the point.

"Because I am," he said. "Because I don't have anyplace else to go, okay?"

"Oh." There was a long pause, then I said softly, "What happened?"

Grady pointed a finger at me. "Oh, no. Not yet. First you've gotta swear you won't tell anybody about this. Nobody."

"Okay. I swear."

But Grady wasn't finished. "Because if anybody finds out I'm up here, I'm going to . . . I'm going to . . ." He thought for a minute. "I'm going to go down to Gifts and tell them who busted that polar bear. Clear?"

I gulped. "But that's more than a year's allowance!"

"I'll do it, too!" he said.

"Okay," I said reluctantly. "I said I wouldn't tell, and I mean it."

We shook on it, fair and square, and then Grady settled himself back on the sleeping bag. "Okay, now what do you want to know?"

"Just why you're here, that's all."

"It's not that complicated," he said. "I wasn't getting along with my old man, so I left."

"You mean you ran away from home?" I'd never met a real runaway. They weren't too common on Lilac Lane.

"It's no big deal. I'm old enough to take care of myself."

"But why? Why don't you get along?"

"We just don't." He shrugged.

"Do you fight?"

He gave an amused smile. "All we do is fight. He yells. I yell back."

"What about?"

Grady thought for a minute. "He sees things his way, and I see them mine."

"That sounds like *my* dad."

Grady shrugged. "It's different."

"Why? I don't get it."

"Because he's pigheaded." Grady shook his head. "I am, too, I guess. And two pigheads under one roof is bad news. I decided after our last big fight that we'd both do better if I wasn't around."

"But what about your mom? Don't you think she's worried about you? What if she's called the police?"

"She knows I'm in the area. . . ." He stared at the TV. "Anyway, she's got my sisters to think about."

"I thought you said you were an only child."

"Oh." There went the eyes. Dart. Dart. "I guess I have two little sisters. Five and six."

No wonder he was shopping in the children's department earlier! I looked around the half-lit room. "How did you ever find this place, anyway?"

"Luck. . . ," said Grady. "It doesn't matter how I ended up here. It's warm. That's what counts."

I wanted to say something helpful, like maybe he and his dad could make up so he wouldn't have to live in Hocker's ceiling, but what came out was, "Well, you can't hide here forever. Sooner or later someone will find you."

Grady reached one bony hand into the popcorn can and groped for another handful. "I'm not planning to." With his other hand, he reached calmly into his back pocket and pulled out a wad of bills. "In another few days I'll have enough saved for a bus ticket to Miami."

"Miami!" I practically croaked. "Does your mom know about this?"

"What's my old lady got to do with it?"

I shook my head. Running away to live in Hocker's was one thing, but running to Miami was something else. "What about school?"

Grady shrugged. "I can always go back once I have a job."

"Where will you stay?"

"I can sleep on the beach until I have enough saved for a place," said Grady.

I wanted to tell him I thought that was a stupid idea, that running away to Miami would only get his picture on a milk carton, or worse, a Wanted poster, but instead I said, "What would happen if you and your dad made up?"

He gave me that disgusted look again. "Where'd you grow up? Candy Land?"

I thought about Mom and Dad and Sarah and decided not to answer.

"Besides, I'm not interested in making up—even if he is." He focused his attention back on the TV. "Now I would appreciate it if you'd keep your mouth shut so I can make as much money as possible before my job ends."

I got up reluctantly, knowing Dad was probably wondering what had happened to me. "Running away doesn't solve anything," I said, knocking my head on the ceiling.

Grady glanced up. "It lets me start over."

"Oh, sure," I said, feeling myself getting mad. "What kind of life starts with sleeping on some beach?"

Grady's eyes narrowed. "It's *my* life, Tinker Bell. Besides, I'm gonna make something of myself. You watch."

I wanted to believe him, especially since it was Christmas, the time of miracles. Something told me, though, that Grady was heading for the finish this time, and not the start.

That night, I dreamed I was living in T. D. Hocker's. I slept each night in one of the different bedroom displays, wearing a fresh nightgown from Lingerie. Each morning before the store opened, I went down and chose a new outfit from Young Teens and put back the outfit from the day before (except for underwear, which is nonreturnable). I had just gotten to the part about what to have for breakfast, gourmet chocolate-chip cookies or scones, when I felt this parched sensation in my mouth and woke up. The clock read 2:46, and I needed a swig of orange juice bad.

I tiptoed down to the fridge and helped myself to the carton, not bothering with a glass since no one was around to yell at me for spreading germs. The ice-cold liquid slid down my throat and landed with a comforting plunk in my stomach.

I stood very still and thought about Grady, asleep in T. D. Hocker's ceiling. What happened if *he* woke up in the middle of the night and wanted a swig of juice? Did he keep extra on hand? Where did he go to brush his teeth or wash his hair or take a shower? What was it like, knowing you couldn't go home? "He's not so tough," I said aloud. "He's as scared as anybody."

"Who?" asked a voice behind me.

I jumped about a mile. "Dad! What are you doing up?"

He grinned. "I heard someone drinking out of the carton."

I looked down at the container. "Oh."

Dad opened the cupboard and took out one of Mom's Christmas cookie tins that she was probably planning to give to someone she hardly knew. "Care to join me?" He gave his belly a jolly pat. "A little extra padding around the holidays never hurt."

I carried two clean glasses and the O.J. over to the table, where Dad was already picking out his favorites, the mint pistachios. "So," he said, handing me a frosted star with sprinkles (*my* favorite). "I heard something distressing about our friend Grady today."

My cookie snapped in half. "Grady Watkins, you mean?"

Dad nodded.

I took a tiny polite bite. "What was it?"

He shook his head. "Can you keep this quiet?"

"Sure."

Dad turned his cookie over several times. "Joanne is thinking of letting him go."

"She can't!" I cried in a voice normally reserved for soccer practice. I cleared my throat and lowered my octave. "Why would she do that? He's on time and he does a good job, doesn't he?"

Dad looked down at the table. "Apparently his behavior outside Santa Land has come under suspicion. Several employees in other departments have reported seeing him act strangely—moving items around the store, sneaking past people. . . . There's some speculation that he might be stealing."

I swallowed. "But no one's *seen* him steal anything, have they?"

"No," said Dad. "I told Joanne that, but she doesn't want to take any chances. She said we don't *really* need the extra help and that she only hired Grady as a favor to me." He sighed. "I tried my best to argue, Megan, but her mind is made up."

I nibbled down the points of my star cookie until all that was left was a small circle. "But Dad, everyone in Santa Land likes him. Besides, he needs the money. He told me."

Dad sighed. "Well, as far as the money goes, maybe I can work something out. . . ."

"And he needs to stay until Christmas, too," I added quickly. Firing Grady and giving him extra pay would be the *worst* thing that could happen. I was sure he'd buy a ticket for the next bus to Miami.

I pressed a few cookie crumbs into the table. "He's not doing anything wrong," I said. "I know he isn't."

"I believe you," said Dad. "Nevertheless, security is starting to keep an extra eye on him." He gave me a look. "By the way, Tom Roberts in Rugs said he ran into you the other day down on five."

Dad really knows how to ruin a good cookie. "Oh."

"Megan, if you need to talk about something, I'm here."

I remembered my promise to Grady. "I know. Everything's fine." I swallowed my cookie circle. We sat quietly for a moment. "It's spooky down here in the dark, don't you think?"

"Mmm-hmm."

"Dad?"

"Yes?"

"I'm glad we don't fight."

Dad laughed. "Not yet, at any rate. You haven't hit puberty."

I felt my face turn red.

"What I meant to say," Dad cut in quickly, "is that some times are easier than others, and that fights don't necessarily mean we don't love each other."

I thought about my fight with Sarah earlier, then wondered whether the same thing applied to Grady's family. They had to care about him more than he thought, didn't they? I pulled out a mint pistachio that was hiding under a wedding cookie. "Here, Dad, last one."

Dad grinned. "I was going to leave that one there in case Mom checked the tin. Ready to head back upstairs?"

I nodded. "Dad?"

"Yes?"

I took a breath and let it out. "I love you."

He gave me a hug. "I love you, too, Meggie. See you in the morning."

Chapter Nine

Grady wasn't scheduled to work again until the next afternoon, so I knew I'd find him in his hideout during my lunch break.

"What are you doing here?" he said with a grumble when I showed up. "I thought I told you to stay away." He was in the same spot I'd seen him in the day before, this time watching an old cowboy movie.

"I know," I said. "But I brought you some lunch." I waved a giant red-and-green T. D. Hocker's shopping bag at him. "I've got real macaroni and cheese in here. It's one of Mom's specialties."

Grady sniffed. "Reminds me of elementary school."

I took it out anyway, along with some peeled carrots, deviled eggs, and tangerines. "At least try it," I said. "It had a chance to warm up in my locker all morning." I handed him the container and a plastic fork.

Grady took a tiny bite. "Not bad." He looked up. "Wait a second! Isn't this macaroni supposed to be red and green?" He looked down at his meal. "Or is today orange-colored foods?"

I felt my cheeks tingle. "She only does color themes for special occasions."

Grady gave me a long look. "You shouldn't be so embarrassed," he said, shrugging. "My mom's specialty is Jell-O molds. Every time she goes to a potluck, she takes one."

He turned back to Mom's macaroni, taking another bite, then another until he was practically shoveling it in. "So, did anybody see you come up here?" he asked between mouthfuls.

"No."

I watched Grady finish the rest of the food, all except for one carrot and a tangerine. "Those are for later," he said, tucking them into a cooler from Housewares.

"I can bring more if you want," I said. "My mom always buys too much of everything." I glanced around. "It must be hard to stay cooped up in here."

"You get used to it."

"Still . . ." I could see he didn't like personal questions, but there was so much I wanted to ask him—especially about his family.

I noticed the denim skirt and vest still next to the roll of wrapping paper and ribbon. "What's it like having little sisters?" I asked. "I always wished I had a sister who didn't act like she was my baby-sitter all the time."

"Nikky and Jessie probably feel the same way about me," said Grady, wiping his fingers on a Santa napkin.

I thought for a minute. "I guess that's what happens when kids are far apart in age."

"Yeah," said Grady. "Built-in baby-sitter. No fun."

I wondered whether Sarah felt the same way. I motioned to the corner. "Is that outfit for one of your sisters?"

Grady barely glanced up. "Nikky. Jessie's getting the jacket."

"That's nice. Is that bottle of perfume for your mom?"

He started to look a little grouchy. "What's it to you?"

"Just wondering, that's all. Seems like you sort of miss them." Grady didn't say anything. "What are you getting your dad?"

"Nothing! Okay?" He turned the TV volume back up. "Isn't your lunch break almost over?"

Subject closed. I started gathering up the empty containers. "I wanted to tell you something. . . ." I gave him a sidelong glance.

"What?"

"Dad told me last night that a few people noticed you moving your things around on the sales floor. They think you might be stealing."

Grady's eyes widened. "I ain't stealing!" He gestured angrily at the pile of gifts in the corner. "I paid for every one of those. . . . Wanna see the receipts?"

"I believe you. Be careful, that's all."

Grady slammed his fist into his sleeping bag.

"What's wrong?"

"What is it about me?" he muttered. "Why can't people leave me alone?"

"They probably would have if you hadn't moved your shopping bags around," I said in a helpful voice. "And anyway, you're sort of hard to miss, you know?"

Grady grunted and gave a half smile.

"Besides, it's not as if people don't like you. If my dad didn't care about you, he wouldn't have mentioned what he'd heard."

"Your old man is reasonable. Mine is not." He went on quietly. "I could even put up with his pigheadedness if I had to. You know why I really can't stand him, though?"

"Why?"

Grady shook his head. "Because he's got no faith in me. I was working as a grocery delivery boy, and the manager accused me of dipping my hand in the register."

"Were you?"

"No way! Grady Watkins is a man to be trusted. Soon as my old man found out about it, though, he told me I would never amount to anything." He gave a sarcastic laugh.

"Why didn't you tell your dad you weren't the one stealing?"

Grady's shoulders straightened, and he looked me right in the eye. "Because he should have known better."

"You're right," I said. "My dad would never have done something like that. He always gives us the benefit of the doubt, no matter what."

"See what I mean?" said Grady.

We sat silently. "Grady?" I said finally.

"Yeah?"

"If you could have anything in the world, what would it be?"

He gave a sigh that sounded like air being let out of a rubber mattress. "Other than a million dollars?"

"Yeah."

He leaned his head back. "I guess I want people to take me seriously. How about you?"

"Well . . ." I thought about Dad and Mom and Sarah and then Trevor Harris. "I guess the same thing."

Grady nodded.

We sat silently, absorbed in our own thoughts. "It's so quiet up here," I said finally.

"I know," said Grady. "Sometimes I wish I could stay forever." He rumpled his hair with his fingers. "So what else did Ed say?"

I bit my lip. "That's it."

"Liar!"

"Look. I've said enough already."

Grady sat up. His hair was all prickly and matted in the back where he'd been lying on his pillow. "You don't have to keep anything from me."

"I'm not." I didn't want to tell him about the possibility of losing his job, especially after the things he'd just said.

Grady put on his tough-guy face. "I can look out for myself."

My eyes narrowed. "Don't be dumb, Grady. If you get caught here, you'll be arrested." I motioned around the room. "Everything you dragged up here belongs to Hocker's, not to mention this building is private property."

"Don't you think I know that?"

"Why do you always have to act so tough?" I said, grabbing my shopping bag. "I was only trying to be your friend."

Grady scowled. "Why don't you mind your own business?"

"I will," I said, crawling off on all fours. Grady started to laugh. Over my shoulder I yelled, "And don't make fun of the way I crawl!"

Mom always says anger bears consequences, so I guess it was my own fault I opened the panel without peeking first. As soon as I straightened up, though, I knew I was in trouble.

Charging in my direction from halfway across the room was the man who had caught me going through his desk. "What are you doing?" he demanded, screeching to a halt in front of me.

Not sure how much he'd seen, I waved my shopping bag and said, "I ate lunch back here. It's nice and quiet." I pulled out the empty container and showed it to him. "Homemade macaroni."

He squinted his eyes as if he wasn't entirely convinced. "But . . . you can't do that. These Persians are for sale."

I tried to appear as apologetic as possible. "Sorry. I promise I didn't drop any crumbs on them."

His eyes wandered suspiciously to the extension cord, plugged into the wall behind me. I quickly took a step to my right to block it from view. "What are you up to, anyway?"

"Nothing. I promise. I'm just on my lunch break."

He leaned to his right. I leaned to my left.

A lady wearing a knit hat came up behind him. "Excuse me," she said. "May I have some help?"

He spun around, all smiles. "Certainly! By all means."

I shot out of there as fast as I could. "I blew it," I muttered, bolting for the escalator. "I blew Grady's cover. I have to warn him."

Once upstairs, I planted myself beside

the time clock, determined not to move until I saw him.

Five minutes passed, then ten. Grady was late. Maybe he was having trouble getting out of his hideout. Maybe the rug man had already caught him. Why hadn't I been more careful? How much had the rug man seen? Finally, I saw Grady come around the corner.

"What do *you* want?" he said as he punched in.

"Where *were* you?"

Grady looked around. "I had a little trouble leaving."

I felt awful. "Did the rug man see you?"

Just as Grady was about to answer, Joanne stepped up. "Grady. You're late."

"Only a few minutes!" I said.

Joanne frowned. "I was talking to Grady, Megan."

"Sorry."

"If you want, I can stay extra," said Grady.

"That won't be necessary," said Joanne crisply. I pictured a huge ax about to fall on Grady's head. "I've been thinking that . . ."

I had to do something. I grabbed Joanne's arm and began moaning. "Ohhhhhh . . ."

"Megan! What is it?"

I clutched at my stomach and moaned again, this time even louder. "I don't feel good. I think I'm going to throw up."

"Step away from the time clock," she said, jumping out of the way herself. "Where's your father?"

I covered my mouth with my hand and gagged a little bit.

"I'll get a wastebasket." She dove into the nearest office.

"Faker," said Grady as soon as she was gone.

"Go get on the train before she fires you, dummy," I hissed.

Grady's eyes almost popped out. "Fires me? What for? I didn't do anything!" He looked totally disgusted. "I've had enough of this place."

"Go to the train, will you?" I gave him a shove.

I turned back around, only to have a large rubber wastebasket shoved under my chin.

"Here, Megan," said Joanne.

I gave her a weak smile. "Thanks." A pitiful cough. "I'm feeling much better."

"Are you sure?"

"Positive."

"Maybe you should take it easy. I can put another elf on in your place."

"You can?" To be honest, I wasn't in the mood to squeak a toy dog. I needed some time to think. So much was happening. "Well . . . I *am* still feeling a tiny bit nauseous. . . ." I put my hand on my stomach again.

Joanne smiled nervously and handed me the wastebasket. "Why don't you go find your father and tell him I'm giving you the rest of the day off? You can lie down on that little cot in the elf dressing room."

Out of the corner of my eye, I could see Grady chugging around the room on the train. Safe for the moment, I figured. "Okay," I said. "Thanks." I handed the wastebasket back to Joanne and hurried off before she had a chance to change her mind.

Chapter Ten

The cot in the elf dressing room was buried beneath a pile of dirty tunics, which I didn't even bother to push aside. Instead I dug myself in under them, just like Jennifer's dachshund, Prunella, would do, and pulled an elf hat down over my eyes. Peace at last. I lay still, blocking out all interfering thoughts.

"How you feeling?"

Sighing, I peeked out from under my elf hat.

"Oh, hi, Marge. Okay, I guess."

"Your dad asked me to check up on you."

"I'm fine."

Elf Marge squeezed herself onto the end of the cot, causing it to give off a major squeak. "The holidays can be very stressful," she said.

"Tell me about it."

"Well, there's all that shopping that has to get done, buying things for people—some of whom you hardly even know—and then of course extra parties, extra activities, extra family around." She gave her stomach a pat and then added with a sigh, "Extra food." She beamed down at me sympathetically. "Sorry to hear about Grady, Megan. I know he was your friend."

I lifted my head. "What about him?"

"Oh." She looked at me like my parakeet had just died. "I thought you'd heard. He just went into Joanne's office and quit."

"You're kidding!" I threw my feet on the floor, knocking Marge and the cot off balance. "He can't do that!"

I flew past Marge and out to the train. "Where's Grady?" I asked Carole as she drove past.

"He left," she shouted. "And this is supposed to be my lunch break."

I pushed my way past the lines and found Joanne next. "Did he really quit?" I asked, bolting into her office.

Joanne looked up from her paperwork. "Megan! I thought you weren't feeling well."

"Now he's gonna leave for sure," I said.

"What are you talking about?"

"It's all my fault. I shouldn't have said anything. I knew it."

"Megan . . . wait!"

I ran back out and headed for five.

"Have you seen that kid Grady?" I asked Oswald as soon as I stepped off the escalator.

"Not today, sugar." It was Mr. Washington again.

I sighed and turned to search the room.

"Why so glum?"

Normally I don't cry in front of grown-ups, but a bear is something else. "I think I blew it," I said, feeling my eyes start to fill up. The next thing I knew, promise or no promise, I was confessing everything to Oswald—how Grady had run away from home, was living in the store, and was now about to leave for Miami, thanks to me. "You won't tell anyone, will you? I swore I wouldn't say anything or else I owe somebody a lot of money."

"Of course not," said Oswald. "We bears know how to keep a secret." A couple of little kids came up behind me and got into line. "You know, Megan. You shouldn't be so hard on yourself. Sounds like Grady had his mind made up a long time ago."

I sucked in a few sniffles. "Yeah, but if I'd had a little more time, I might have been able to change it."

"Some kids need to learn things the hard way."

"But that's giving up on him."

Oswald paused. "True." The line behind me was growing larger. "Let me take care of this group so we can talk some more, okay?"

I stood to one side and listened quietly as Oswald began to sing "Silent Night." I got all choked up again. Here it was, nearly Christmas, and nothing seemed calm *or* bright, especially since . . . I gasped. "Oh no!" Across the room I saw two men in uniform heading for the rug department.

"Mr. Washington!" I hissed. He was on his last heavenly pe-eace. "Emergency! Two security guards are heading for Rugs. They've got flashlights."

"Bye now," Oswald said to the kids. "Be sure and stop by to see Santa Claus, you hear?"

I pressed my mouth against the side of the metal booth. "Mr. Washington!" I whispered through the wall. "We have to do something. If they find Grady's hideout, he'll be arrested."

"I don't want any trouble," he said.

Now the guards were shining their flashlights up and down the ceiling. "I know. All you have to do is distract the guards."

The next thing I knew, Mr. Washington had opened the door and was peeping out at me from behind the booth. "I'd like to help you, sugar, but I'm not supposed to leave the box."

The security guards approached the rug man. "What if I watched it for you? Nobody's around now, anyway."

Mr. Washington didn't look too sure. "Well . . ."

"It's only for a minute. Please? If I go over there, the rug man will know something's up. He already suspects me. Please? The least we can do is give Grady a chance to escape."

Mr. Washington shook his head, then stepped aside. "Okay. Get inside till I come back. I'll see what I can do."

I scooted in and heard the heavy metal door slam behind me. The booth was cramped and dark, with barely enough room for its one tall stool and the long curtains that separated me from Oswald. Carefully I climbed up and peeped through the curtains. "Wow."

Even though the back of Oswald's head blocked my view a little, I still had a good shot of the sales floor, including Mr. Washington, who had already made it to the other side of the room. I could see him saying something to the security guards, waving his long arms up and down and pointing toward the escalator. Whatever he said must have worked because the guards both turned and followed him in that direction.

Suddenly my view was blocked by two familiar brown eyes. "Hi, Oswald."

Oh no! I quickly pulled my head back.

"Anybody home?" said the voice.

I carefully peeked out. Either this was one of those weird dreams that feels real or else I really did have the worst luck in the world. Standing on the other side of the Oswald booth were none other than Trevor Harris and his four-year-old brother, Ian. "Yo. Are you there?" Trevor said. He banged on the window again. "Hey, Oswald. Why don't you answer?"

"Let *me* have a turn now," said Ian. "I can't see. Move over."

What could I do? I had to say something, right? Mr. Washington was counting on me. Now Ian began banging. "Hello, hello?" he shouted. Jeez Louise! I peeped out. Trevor was holding Ian up in front of Oswald's face, but I knew neither one of them could see me. They'd never know who it was. Never.

I took a deep breath, grabbed the two big pincers that move Oswald's mouth, and said in my deepest voice, "'Course I'm here. Hello, Ian, hello, Trevor."

When Trevor heard his name, he stepped back and laughed uncomfortably. "Hey. How'd you know my name?"

I smiled to myself and moved Oswald's mouth again. "The mighty Oswald knows everyone. Isn't that right, Ian?"

Ian turned gray and buried his head in Trevor's shoulder. Trevor looked a little embarrassed. "Come on, Ian. Stop."

"Don't worry," I said quickly. "I don't bite. I'm a friendly ol' bear. Yuk, yuk."

Ian turned and smiled shyly. "Will you sing 'Jingle Bell Rock'?"

Uh-oh. Being able to carry a tune isn't one of my talents. "Um, Oswald's got a sore throat today," I said. "I took a long walk in the forest yesterday without my jacket and caught a slight cold." Ian nodded, satisfied. I guess maybe my father's genes were heating up.

Trevor kept looking at Oswald funny. "What else do you know about me?"

"Plenty."

"Like what?"

I couldn't help it. "Like . . . you live on Ward Street," I said. "Like you have Mrs. Perry for homeroom, like you went to Camp Wishbone last summer, like your mother's name is *Dorinda*. . . ." It was getting hard not to laugh.

Trevor pressed closer. "Hey! Who is this, anyway?"

I laughed to myself but kept Oswald's mouth moving. "I am Oswald, talking bear extraordinaire." I wished Jennifer could see me now. This was better than *The Wizard of Oz*. I glanced over at Mr. Washington. He and the security people were still by the escalators. "Have you been up to six yet to visit Santa Claus?" I said, remembering Oswald's manners.

"Yeah," said Trevor, still staring at Oswald. I could tell the mystery was killing him.

I noticed Trevor's parents approaching. "Look! There's Tom and Dorinda now."

Trevor smiled nervously.

"Ready, boys?" said Mrs. Harris.

"Oswald knows our names," Ian told her. "And a lot of other stuff."

"Really?" said Mrs. Harris.

"That's right," I said. As proof, I was tempted to bring up the time she accidentally ran over the school-crossing sign, but then I thought better of it. Besides, I could see Mr. Washington heading back. "Thanks for stopping by," I made Oswald say.

They started to walk off, then Trevor came racing back. "Who are you *really*?" he asked.

"I already told you," I said, letting the make-believe rub in. "I'm Oswald, the talking bear."

"You sound like a kid," said Trevor.

"Well . . . there's a little bit of kid inside every bear," I said. Trevor gave me another penetrating stare, but by now I was feeling invincible. No wonder Dad likes his job, I thought. Being inside Oswald is probably no different than being inside Santa. It's all part of the same pretend.

"Why, hello there, Oswald," said Mr. Washington, coming directly into view. He gave me a giant smile and then said to Trevor, "On your way up to see Santa, young man?"

Trevor shook his head and started to go, but not before glancing back once more. "So long," I called after him. When I was sure he was out of earshot, I added under my breath, "You cute thing."

Mr. Washington cleared his throat. "Friend of yours?"

"Sort of."

"Nice-lookin' boy."

"I know. . . ." I wondered whether Trevor and I would ever have a normal encounter. "What happened with the security guards?"

"Sent 'em downstairs. They'll be back tomorrow, though. They're curious about that extension cord. Tell Grady it's time to find another hotel."

"He's probably up there packing now," I said miserably.

Mr. Washington smiled. "You know, Megan, I've been thinking about what you said earlier—about not wanting to give up. It never hurts to keep trying, especially if you believe what you're doing is right."

"Thanks," I said.

Mr. Washington looked over his shoulder. "Ooops. Customer coming. Time for you to skedaddle, Madame Bear."

I opened the door and traded places with Mr. Washington.

He squeezed my hand. "Be sure to tell me what happens, will you? We bears like to stick together."

I smiled. "Okay, Oswald." Unsure of what my next move should be, I headed back to the elf dressing room to regroup.

Chapter Eleven

I was barely off the escalator when Joanne came rushing over. "Megan! Are you all right? Where've you been?"

"Downstairs . . ."

Her eyebrows crinkled up. "We've all been worried about you. Marge said you were upset about Grady."

I nodded. "He knew you were planning to fire him, so he quit."

"Oh, Megan. I'm sorry to lose Grady, I really am. Everyone thought he was delightful, but it's probably just as well."

"He needs a job," I said.

Joanne smiled sympathetically. "Well, I'm sure he'll be able to find something else. He's a very resourceful young man." I didn't say anything. Joanne stared at me intently. "How are you feeling?"

"Better."

She seemed relieved. "Oh, good. Then I have a huge favor to ask. One of my elves didn't show up in room one. Think you can help out? I don't want to force you, but I'd really appreciate it." She motioned to the line, which was jammed with people. "We're so busy."

"Well . . ." I looked around reluctantly. Where *was* Grady? "I have to change first."

Joanne smiled and started toward the Gingerbread House. "Great. I do appreciate this. I'm having some day." I started to follow her inside when something caught my eye. "I'll be there in a minute," I called.

I walked over to one of the displays near the Santa Land entrance. This one was a kid-size scene of two lifelike mechanical bears sitting at a little table and drinking hot cocoa. Only now a third had joined the party.

I stepped over the velvet roping and sat down beside the bears' uninvited guest. "Hi, Ian. What'cha doing?"

Ian turned to me with a serious expression. "Talking." He leaned over and put his arm around the bear with the green striped vest. "Want some more cookies, Bill?"

I looked around the room. "Where's your mom?"

Ian gave me a blank look.

"Okay . . . Where's Trevor?"

"Trevor's dumb. He's a big bully."

"I bet he's wondering where you are right now."

"Finish your juice, Suzie," Ian told the other bear. He turned to me. "Want some pie?"

"What kind?"

"Spinach and slop."

"Mmm, my favorite," I said, pretending to gobble some down. Ian cracked up.

An angry voice interrupted our tea party. "Ian Harris! Don't ever run away from me like that again. If Mom and Dad knew, they'd be freaking out. I thought you'd been kidnapped!"

Then he noticed me. "Oh no! Not you again!"

This wasn't exactly the normal encounter I'd hoped for, but at least I wasn't sitting inside a bear or wearing my elf costume. "Oh! Hi, Trevor," I said as calmly as possible.

"What are you doing to my brother?" asked Trevor. He immediately leaned down and snatched Ian off the floor, causing the poor kid to launch into a relentless series of wails.

"Wait a second," I said, springing to my

own defense. "For your information, I was the one who found him."

"Then why's he crying?" shouted Trevor over the noise.

"I want those bears," Ian wailed. "Put me down!"

"Yeah! Put him down," I shouted.

"Oh, okay," said Trevor, more than a little annoyed. The instant Ian's feet hit the ground, there was silence.

"I'm back, bears," said Ian, immediately settling himself at the table again. "Please pass the juice, Bill."

I was left standing face-to-face with Trevor. "I can't believe you would accuse me of kidnapping," I said in my iciest voice.

"Sorry," said Trevor. "Do you know how scary it is to lose a little kid?"

"He only wanted to talk to the bears," I said. Without thinking I added, "I guess he thinks they're real."

A startled expression crossed Trevor's face.

"I mean . . . you know how little kids like to pretend."

"But he can't just run off," said Trevor, recovering. "I'm in charge of him. What if something happened?"

"Nothing did," I said.

Trevor frowned. Cutely. "What are you doing here, anyway?"

"Um. Well." Looking into those eyes made me completely melt. "I sort of work here."

"Doing what?"

I don't know what came over me. Christmas dust? "I'm helping my dad." I lowered my voice to keep Ian from overhearing. "He's the head Santa here."

"He is?" said Trevor. "Wow."

Good move, Megan, I told myself. "And that reminds me," I said aloud. "I've gotta go. I'm supposed to be on duty now." I crouched down beside Ian, who was telling one of the bears his Christmas list. "Bye. Thanks for the pie."

"Grrr," said Ian.

I leaned over and whispered into his ear. "I bet Trevor would like to try a slice. Why don't you ask him?" Ian made a silly face and giggled.

I stood back up. "See you around."

"Okay!" said Trevor. "Okay!"

I took that as a very good sign. Maybe even a yes.

Three very long hours later, I was finally set free. Joanne had assigned me to the Santa Dad calls the Born-Again Santa, the one with the real beard and motorcycle boots whose Sunday School class had persuaded him to try out for the part. When I first checked in, all I could think about was Trevor, Trevor, Trevor. As time went on, though, I began to worry about Grady again. If I could only speak to him, tell him once more what I thought about his going to Miami. But what if he'd already left? Then what?

When my time was finally up, I dashed to the escalator, anxious to check back with Oswald.

Luckily, Mr. Washington was still on duty. "Anything happen while I was gone?" I asked him.

"Very quiet," he answered.

"No Grady?"

"Nope."

"No security?"

"Nope."

"I've got to find him. . . ," I said, starting for the rug department. Just then I saw Sarah stomping her way over. "Megan? Where'd you go? Dad and I have been waiting for you for an hour! He has a party in forty-five minutes and he still has to drop us off at home." Here we go again, I thought.

"Didn't Joanne tell you? I was helping the Born-Again Santa."

"Well, it's time to go home now."

I looked around wildly. "I can't."

"Why not?"

"Because I can't."

Sarah put her hands on her hips. "Megan! What's with you?"

"I have to do something first. Tell Dad I'll be up in a minute." I looked at her. "Do you have a piece of paper and a pencil I can borrow?"

She stared at me for a moment, then began leafing through her bag. "You've gotten very weird lately," she said, handing me a little decorated paper pad with a pencil attached.

"Sarah," I said. "I'm not a little kid anymore."

"What's that supposed to mean?"

"I realize it's always been your job to look after me, but I'm in middle school now. I'm old enough to baby-sit. I'm old enough to go to the mall by myself. I'm practically a teenager."

Sarah squinted.

"Don't tell Mom and Dad, but I even have a sort of boyfriend. He's an eighth grader."

"Really?" said Sarah. I could tell this information was casting me in a whole new light.

"Really," I said. "I'll be up in three minutes."

"Okay," said Sarah. She turned to leave, but not before looking peculiarly at me once more.

Leaning against one of the counters, I wrote, "Dear Grady, I still don't think you should leave. Your friend, Megan."

I sidled over to Rugs, then carefully made sure no one was watching before hanging the note on one of the ladder rungs inside the panel. There. At least I'd tried. At least Grady would know there was one person who wasn't giving up on him.

Dad and Sarah were waiting for me upstairs in the back hall, since Dad was still in costume. "Ready?" he said.

"Ready," I answered. Swallowing hard, I followed the two of them to the freight elevators.

Dad and Sarah sang "The Twelve Days of Christmas" on the way home. Twice. All I could think about, though, was how maybe I could have done more for Grady. But what?

We pulled into the driveway and sat for a moment, admiring the lights. "Pretty, huh?" said Dad.

"Yeah," Sarah and I answered in unison.

We laughed, then followed Dad into the house.

I didn't feel much like hanging around the family room, so I went up to my bedroom and shut the door. Maybe this was a good time to finish wrapping my presents.

I hadn't even pulled my gifts out from underneath the bed when I heard a knock. "Who is it?"

"Me. Why so glum, chum?" said Dad, walking in. Downstairs, "Here Comes Santa Claus" had started playing on the stereo. Dad joined in, mouthing the words and bouncing around my room in his costume like an overstuffed blimp. As I watched him hopping around, it suddenly became clear to me what I needed to do. There was no other solution. Christmas is a time of miracles, and if Grady wouldn't listen to me, maybe—just maybe—he'd listen to Santa.

I knew it meant the end of allowance for the rest of my middle-school career. I knew it was taking a big chance. But I also knew that if anyone represented hope, it was Santa. I shivered. What was happening to me? A few weeks ago, all hope had meant was scuba gear and all Santa had meant was Dad in a goofy costume.

"Santa," I said slowly. "I have something to ask you, and it's very important."

I guess the whole story was bound to come out sooner or later, promise or no promise. What I didn't expect, though, was for Dad to grab my coat and pull me back out to the car.

"Wait. Where are we going?"

Dad looked grim. "To Hocker's. I'd like to try and talk to Grady if he hasn't already left."

"But Hocker's is closed. And what about your party?"

"The night watchman will let me in. And I can be a few minutes late to the party. It doesn't really get going for another half hour or so."

We drove along in silence. "Dad," I said finally. "What are you going to do?"

"I'm not sure yet."

"Are you mad at me for not telling you about Grady sooner?"

"Of course not."

"It's just that if Santa can't help, who can?"

We parked the car by the loading dock and rang the night bell.

"Well, if it ain't Santa Claus!" said the watchman when he opened the door.

"Hi, Columbus," said Dad. "Mind if we

go upstairs? I forgot something." He gave me a wink.

The door swung open. "Surely," said Columbus, bowing. "Anything for Mr. Claus."

We took the elevator to five since the escalators were turned off. "Wow," I said, stepping onto the showroom floor. Except for the occasional sparkle of a Christmas decoration, everything was dark and still.

"You're the leader," said Dad.

I gave him a funny look. Here in the dim light, if I squinted my eyes shut, I could almost imagine he was the real thing.

"What is it?" asked Dad.

I blinked. "Nothing."

Dad gently took my shoulders. "Remember, Megan. Santa can't always do everything."

"I know."

He straightened up. "Where to, kiddo?"

"This way." We tiptoed past Linens and through Rugs until we came to the panel. "In here," I said, pushing it back. My heart gave a skip. The note was gone. Maybe Grady was still around.

With a little help, Dad managed to squeeze inside.

"We have to climb up this ladder and

then crawl for a while," I told him. "Think you can make it?"

He gave his belly a pat. "If my padding cooperates."

This time there were no noises coming from the back. No flickering light. "Grady," I called softly. "Are you there? It's me. Megan."

We crawled along slowly. "Megan," grunted Dad. "How in the world did you find this place?"

"Yoo-hoo. Grady." We rounded the last corner. I took a sharp breath.

The sleeping bags, the TV, the cooler . . . all of it was gone.

Then in the far corner, I saw a large lump move. "Grady?"

"Huh?" The lump sat up. "Who is it?" A flashlight beamed into my eyes.

"It's me. Megan. I brought Dad."

"Hi, son," said Dad. "It's Santa."

Grady scowled. "What are you doing here? What do you want?"

"Did you get my note?" I said, inching closer.

Grady tugged at his grubby-looking blanket. "You promised!" he said.

"I know all about the polar bear," interrupted Dad. "Megan is prepared to pay for it."

Grady gave me an incredulous look. "You are? Why would you do a stupid thing like that?"

"I hear you're leaving," said Dad.

Grady pulled the blanket over his head and rolled back over. "That's right."

"Can you tell me what's keeping you from going home?" Dad asked.

Grady didn't answer.

"Grady?"

He swung his head up. "Listen. I don't get along so good with my dad."

Dad cleared his throat. "Grady. I know it's very tough to get along sometimes, maybe even impossible. But I'm sure your father cares about you more than you think."

"Not true," said the lump. "He doesn't care."

Dad drummed his fingers on the floor. "Well, I do. And Megan does. And I think it's pretty special to have someone like Megan willing to go out on a limb for you. Grady, what's important is having people who care. Who's waiting for you in Miami?"

Grady shrugged. "I'll make new friends."

"I have another idea," Dad said. "Stick around. Finish school. You know we're not going to leave you high and dry. Megan's here.

I'm here. When I'm not in this suit I'm Ed Gallagher in Ladies' Shoes. And I'm always around, nine to five, Monday to Friday, if you need to talk or cool out."

Grady stared at Dad, expressionless.

"Grady!" I shouted. "Say something! Don't you get it?" I couldn't believe it. For the first time ever, Mr. Make-Believe—Mr. Never Admit Your Identity While in Costume—was blowing his cover for somebody, and the only response he was getting was a big fat zero. I wanted to grab Grady by the shoulders and shake him.

"I've got nothin' to say," Grady finally answered.

That did it. "I don't believe you," I said. "How do you expect anyone to take a chance on you if you won't take a chance on them? Talk about pigheaded!"

Dad put out his arm and pulled me back. "Megan . . ."

Grady's eyes flashed. "It's my life, okay? Don't tell me what to do."

Dad sighed, then moved back onto his knees. "Well, you think about what we said, okay? We're a sure thing. Miami isn't. I hope we'll see you in the morning."

Chapter Twelve

Oh man! Was I mad! What an ingrate! I stomped all the way back to the car, wishing Grady would fall into a swamp and be eaten alive by a six-foot alligator. "He doesn't deserve you, Dad," I said, sliding into the passenger side and reaching across to pat his knee.

Dad gave my hand a squeeze. "Or you, either. Don't worry, though. Santa never takes these things personally, and neither should you."

"But he was rude to you. I'm sorry I made you go up there."

Dad started the ignition. "Don't be. You did a good thing, Megan, whatever happens. It's important to care about others."

I sighed deeply. "I must have accidentally waded through some Christmas dust this year."

Dad smiled, then slowly backed the car away from the loading dock and turned onto

Meridian Boulevard. "That's my kid," he said.

We rode in silence the rest of the way home.

When we pulled into the driveway, I said, "Dad, can we keep this quiet? I don't feel like telling Mom or Sarah."

"Don't worry," said Dad. "This is between us."

Suddenly Mom came flying out the front door. "There you are!" She leaned her head inside the car window. "Megan, the phone's for you."

I went inside and picked up the receiver. "Hello."

"Megan? It's me. Jennifer! *What* did you tell Trevor?"

"About what?"

"He said he saw you at Hocker's today and that he thinks you're mysterious and strange."

"I am," I said. I thought for a moment. "Is that good or bad?"

"It must be good," said Jennifer. "He wants to ask you to Carmen's skating party next week."

"He does?" I took a big breath. "Jennifer, could you hold on for a minute?" I rested the receiver on the table and screamed. "Aaaaaa!"

Sarah ran in from the next room. "Megan! Are you okay? Why are you screaming?"

I guess it was pretty obvious there was no medical emergency. I grabbed both her hands and began hopping up and down. "I have a date, I have a date," I sang. "With that eighth grader."

"And Mom's letting you go?" asked Sarah incredulously.

Instantly my feet went from a bounce to a brick. Thud. "I hadn't gotten to that part yet," I confessed. I started to pick up the receiver again, now considerably less enthusiastic.

"Maybe," Sarah said, taking my arm, "maybe I can say something to Mom, to sort of warn her before the fact."

"You can?"

"Sure." Then she whispered, "Don't tell Mom, but I went on a date once without her permission when I was twelve."

I was shocked. "You did? I always thought you were perfect."

Sarah smiled. "I know."

I spent that night dreaming about Trevor Harris, which isn't a bad way to spend the night before Christmas Eve. The next morning Dad and I were on our way back to Hocker's, though, and neither of us mentioned Grady the whole trip.

I could tell it was on both our minds, stuck there like an incomplete grade on a report card. When we stepped off the escalator on five, the first thing we noticed were three security people over in Rugs, talking among themselves.

Dad didn't waste any time. "Good morning, gentlemen," he said, walking up to them. "What's going on here?"

I looked around for Grady, fully expecting to see him standing in the corner, handcuffed.

"Seems someone was fooling around up in the crawl space," said one of the guards. He shined his flashlight first at the ladder then at me.

Nailed. My stomach did a triple back flip.

Dad nodded casually. "No kidding? You found someone up there?"

To my complete surprise, the guard shook his head. "Nah. Only a few kernels of popcorn and a smelly blanket. No harm done." He gestured at the panel. "We're going to have to close this thing up, though, so it doesn't happen again."

I crept over to the door and peered up.

"Stay away from there, young lady."

I felt Dad's hands on my shoulders. "Come along," he said, gently steering me away.

When we were back on the escalator, I

said, "Well, at least we know he's not in juvenile hall."

"He might still show up," said Dad.

I don't know. Maybe it was the end of the season, or maybe he was just trying to prepare me for the worst, but Dad's jolliness meter seemed to be flagging. "You really think he might?"

"Megan, please!" He stared straight ahead. "Show some respect for the suit."

"Sorry, Dad." I gently took his hand, and together we stepped off the escalator.

The last few days before Christmas had gotten very quiet around Santa Land; I guess because most parents like to get their Santa shopping done early. Most of our customers now were repeats, here because they'd forgotten to ask for something crucial or because their parents happened to notice the Santa line looked short.

Only thirty people dropped in to see us all morning. And not one of them was Grady.

At one o'clock, Dad stood up and stretched. "Time to go, honey."

"Are you sure?" I stared at the door one last time, like a superhero with X-ray vision, and tried to will Grady through it.

"I'm afraid so." Dad turned to open the

other door, the one leading into the back hall. "Megan, come on."

"Okay." I turned reluctantly and followed him out. "I'll meet you by the elevators."

By this point in the season the dressing room was a complete wreck. I made my way inside and pulled open my locker.

It was on the top shelf, crammed between my purple gloves and my blue sweater. A small white envelope addressed to me. I pulled it down.

The note inside had handwriting so crooked I could hardly read it at first:

Megan, I got to thinking. Two heads are better than one. Two friends are better than none. I guess I'll be seeing you guys around. Sinsearly, Grady W. Watkins. Home phone number 555-1808. P.S. Don't worry about paying for that polar bear. I used my ticket money for it. P.P.S. Merry Christmas. Ho, ho, ho.

I stared at Grady's note for a long time before folding it up and putting it back inside the envelope. Then, using an old pencil stub I found on the dressing room floor, I carefully crossed out my name and wrote: "To Santa. Merry Christmas and love from Megan."